IRON SKY

BOOK 1

DREAD EAGLE

ALEX WOOLF

SCRIBO
A division of Book House

First published in Great Britain by Scribo MMXV
Scribo, a division of Book House, an imprint of
The Salariya Book Company
25 Marlborough Place, Brighton, BN1 1UB
www.salariya.com

ISBN 978-1-909645-00-4

The right of Alex Woolf to be identified as the author of this work has been asserted
in accordance with sections 77 and 78 of the Copyright, Designs
and Patents Act, 1988.

Book Design by David Salariya

© The Salariya Book Company
MMXV

Printed and bound in China

The text for this book is set in Cochin
The display type is GRK1 Ivy No. 2

www.scribobooks.com

Artwork Credits
Front cover illustration: Matthew Laznicka
Gatefold illustrations: Mark Bergin
Map: Carolyn Franklin
Video stills: Jonathan Salariya
Technical wizardry: Mark Williams, Rob Walker

Scan to see the Youtube video

IRON SKY

BOOK 1

DREAD EAGLE

ALEX WOOLF

A division of Book House

IRON SKY · DREAD EAGLE

Folkestone

Brighton

Shoreham
Airport

GREAT BRITAIN

Preston
Weymouth

ENGLISH CHANNEL

FRANCE

Paris

Granville

1. Location of attack on HMAS Borealis
2. Location of Taranis when discovered by Beatrice

N E S W

PROLOGUE

Soon shall thy arm, unconquer'd steam! afar
Drag the slow barge, or drive the rapid car,
Or on wide-waving wings expanded bear
The flying chariot through the fields of air.

Erasmus Darwin, 1781

1 MAY 1845

N apoleon Bonaparte stood upon the steel gantry high above the factory floor. In the claw of his arthritic hand, where once he had wielded a sword, he now clutched the bulb of his walking stick. He was seventy-five years old, and looked it. Yet, despite the extra weight, the silver hair and sagging, grey face, there remained something about him – something in the piercing strength of his dark eyes – that recalled the young man who first bestrode the world half a century ago.

The tour guide gestured with his hand at the view beyond the gantry railing. 'Behold, *Titan*!' he declared theatrically. 'When she is ready in four weeks' time, she will be the largest, most powerful warcraft that ever took to the skies.'

Napoleon surveyed the view with the same steely concentration he once used to study troop formations on the eve of battle. The cathedral-sized hall was dominated by the immense metal frame of an airship, suspended from the roof by gigantic hydraulic arms. Hundreds of ant-sized workers laboured on the wooden scaffolding that covered much of the structure. Huge cranes lifted iron girders up to the scaffolding platforms. Men strapped into harnesses dangling from the roof clambered over the giant airship skeleton, welding the girders into place and sending glittering showers of sparks towards the distant floor.

Napoleon turned to his Minister of Foreign Affairs, who had reluctantly accompanied him on the tour. Talleyrand, who was even older than Napoleon, had for many years been obliged to use to a wheelchair. Napoleon had to raise his voice in order to make himself heard above the deafening whine and clatter of tools. 'I brought you here, my friend,' he shouted, 'so you can see with your own eyes the progress we have made.'

'Impressive,' nodded Talleyrand wearily. 'But I still maintain that the timing is all wrong for an invasion of Britain.'

'The timing will never be right as far as you are concerned!' bellowed Napoleon. 'I may be dead in a year, or even a month, so my doctors keep telling me. If I must wait until you say we are ready, I will be leading the invasion in a hearse!'

'We have enough problems in our own back yard,' persisted Talleyrand. 'We don't need another foreign adventure. There are nationalist mobs on the streets of Vienna, Prague and Madrid, demanding bread and political rights. We could be facing another 1830...'

'The people will never be satisfied!' thundered Napoleon. 'I've given them justice, freedom, education. I've given them the Code Napoléon. What more can they possibly want?'

'Food in their bellies,' murmured Talleyrand.

'Well, we shall give them food soon enough – stripped from the bountiful earth of Kent, Sussex and Hampshire.'

'And you think the British will simply yield this territory to us?'

Napoleon gestured to the airship before them. 'They will have no choice – especially when *Titan* wears the Aetheric Shield. Dressed in her shield of immortality, this great ship will carry the invasion to the very heart of the British Empire: the City of London. We'll blast Nelson's Column from the skies!' He looked charmed by the thought. 'That will be sweet revenge for Trafalgar!'

The tour guide, who had been listening carefully to every word of this conversation, now handed out helmets to Napoleon, Talleyrand and their personal bodyguards. 'Would your excellencies care for a tour of the factory floor?' he asked, guiding the four distinguished visitors gently in the direction of an elevator. 'I can show you where the gondola is being constructed. Now *that* is a sight to behold!'

In a room not far away, the real tour guide had been tied securely to a chair, his cries of anguish muffled by a gag. Later that evening, the impostor, better known in espionage circles as Agent Z, would be sending in a new report to his contact in the British Imperial Secret Service.

PART I

1 JUNE 1845

CHAPTER ONE

THE
AVIATRIX

Lady Arabella West was struggling to stay in control of her aerial steam carriage, which was bucking and rolling around the sky like an unruly colt. Storm clouds loomed above her like dark mountains, their swirling flanks haloed silver in the moonlight. 'Easy, *Prince*,' she whispered, as the wind shuddered through the slender fuselage. 'We'll be down soon.'

Arabella was eighteen years old, with six years of flying experience behind her. Yet tonight, the sky seemed a vast, alien place – she had rarely felt so vulnerable or alone. Beneath the howl of the gale she could hear the soft chug of the engine as her little craft, *Comanche Prince*, bravely, stutteringly fought its way on. In hopes of a smoother flight, Arabella nudged the control stick forward, lowering the elevators on the tail. *Prince*'s nose dropped, and soon the clouds parted beneath them.

From her cockpit window Arabella glimpsed, spread out across the dim landscape below, the glittering spiderweb of lights that was Paris – the enemy capital. Further south, near Fontainebleau, lay the secret airfield that was her destination. She hoped her contact from FAB would be there, as arranged, to light the runway beacons. FAB, the Front Anti-Bonapartiste, were her French friends – they hated Napoleon and were working to help the British win the war.

Beneath the storm, flying was easier, but also much more dangerous. Her altitude was now less than 1,000 feet, well within range of the search beams that crawled across the sky like pale, groping fingers, faintly illuminating the undersides of the storm clouds. If she was caught by one of those lights, she'd become a sitting target for the city's anti-aircraft gunners. She banked right to avoid one. The engine sputtered, and she released the controls for a moment to feed some more coal dust into the burner.

Then she saw it, sailing towards her through wisps of cloud: a long, dark shape, sleek and silent – lethal as a shark. Arabella shivered. The airship's tail bore the insignia of the French Imperial Air Force. She recognised it as a *Tirailleur*-class battlecruiser, lightly armoured and fast. It was less than 500 yards away and closing. She had been spotted! Even as she looked, she saw the guns on the gondola's lower deck taking aim. Arabella rolled and dived as the air began to hiss and crack around her.

Prince rose and dipped through the clouds like a dolphin. He dodged and weaved and spiralled through the sky as shells burst around him. Arabella's hands were in constant movement, gently nudging the control stick, adjusting the ailerons on the wings as her feet applied equally subtle pressure to the rudder pedals. She felt a deep throb of laughter in her chest as she imagined the puzzled Gallic expressions on board the chasing *Tirailleur*.

Qu'est-ce que c'était? Un oiseau?

No one could fly like Arabella. She had been taught by her father, Lord Alfred West, when she was twelve, and almost from day one he had known she was a natural. It was an instinct with her – something she couldn't explain. At times, *Prince* almost seemed like an extension of her body – there was this flow of understanding that passed continuously between them. Father had been a spy, like her. He'd died on a mission in Paris when she was fifteen. Sometimes she thought her only reason for joining the flying corps of the British Imperial Secret Service was to feel closer to him. And at times like these, up here in the sky, she really did. Wherever he was now, she hoped he was watching and was proud of her – proud because he believed, as she did, in doing his duty to his country – whether he agreed with all his country's actions or not.

Arabella knew her father hated the war between Britain and France. He hated the waste of lives and resources on a conflict that had been going on for so long, no one could remember why they were even fighting. In the thirty years that had passed since Napoleon's triumph at Waterloo, neither Britain nor France had won a single decisive battlefield victory. Instead, the world's two remaining superpowers had slugged it out in a long and bloody war of attrition. Fathers had given way to sons in the regiments as the two empires continued to circle each other, like a pair of ageing, punch-drunk prizefighters, neither possessing the energy to land a killer blow.

Sometimes Arabella tried to imagine what it might be like to be at peace with France – its people her friends rather than deadly enemies, their country a destination for a holiday rather than a place where she could expect imprisonment, torture or death. One day, might she fly through these skies as a tourist instead of a spy forced to flee an enemy battlecruiser? It seemed an impossible dream.

The *Tirailleur* was now far behind her, its guns no louder than the crackle of static on her aethercell communicator. Arabella smiled to herself as she pulled out of the spiral, checking her bearings on the gyroscope.

Then her smile faded.

A shadow had fallen across the cockpit, deeper even than the storm clouds. A drone like a billion bees filled her ears. Swallowing, she raised her eyes. She was looking up into the ironclad belly of a *Volcan*-class battlecruiser.

How unfortunate to run into two French warcraft in a single mission – especially when one of them turned out to be a *Volcan*! Almost twice the size of the *Tirailleur*, this was one of the largest and most heavily armoured craft in the French Imperial Fleet. Its gas envelope was entirely encased in an iron exoskeleton. To Arabella, it looked like a gigantic airborne beetle. She blinked as the ship's search beams locked on to her, flooding her tiny cockpit with garish light. Now she was doomed. She could outpace and outmanoeuvre the enormous craft, but no amount of aerobatic trickery could get her out of range of the *Volcan*'s guns. They would pick her off at their leisure, like a frog catching a fly with a lazy flick of its long tongue.

Arabella opened up the throttle valve, sending a surge of power rippling through the air carriage. She banked at 45 degrees and headed west, knowing in her heart it was too late. A thud sounded behind her, like Goliath's boot slamming into the earth. A heart-stopping bang near her port wing sent *Prince* spinning sideways, out of control. She fell hard against the cockpit wall like a wobble-headed doll as a smell of burning filled her nostrils. Had she been hit?

As *Prince* slowly righted himself, from above there came a deafening squeal of heavily amplified speakers, and an echoing, French-accented voice boomed: 'Are you ready for death, English spy?'

Feeling dazed and defeated, Arabella plucked the daguerreotype image of her father from where it was pinned above the control panel, and kissed it. She was ready to die as he had, in the service of her country.

'I'll see you very soon, Father,' she sobbed.

CHAPTER TWO

THE LOGICAL ENGLISHMAN

Arabella sped away from the *Volcan*, every muscle tense as she waited for the inevitable boom of its guns – almost certainly the last sound she would ever hear.

But the boom didn't come.

Instead, her eyes were seared by a purplish-white flash, even brighter than the *Volcan*'s search beam. This was followed by a gargantuan ripping noise, as if the whole sky were a tent and someone were tearing a hole in it.

She heard – and felt – an explosion, its shock wave causing *Prince* to bounce and yaw briefly from side to side. Craning her neck to look up and behind, Arabella glimpsed the *Volcan*, wreathed in smoke and flame. She realised then that the flash had been a bolt of lightning which had struck the great battlecruiser. It must have penetrated the craft's exoskeleton and ignited the hydrogen inside the gas envelope.

Someone up there was watching over her. (*Father!*)

Red-hot debris – the remains of the *Volcan* – fountained through the air all around her as she sped from the scene. *Prince* had scorch marks on his wings, but his engine, thank heavens, felt and sounded OK. Beneath his nosecone, far below, like a miraculous vision, she glimpsed two parallel lines of lights – the secret landing ground she had been heading for. She began her descent.

Ten minutes later, Arabella touched down. *Prince* bounced briefly before his wheels found a firmer grip on the turf. The field to which FAB had guided Arabella was a rutted meadow surrounded by forest. In her line of work she was quite used to bumpy landings in dark fields, but they still unnerved her. One badly placed boulder could smash her wheel, leaving her stranded behind enemy lines. But tonight, at least, the gods seemed to be smiling on her: she came safely to a stop in the corner of the field and shut off her engine.

Raising her flying goggles as she climbed out of the cockpit onto the starboard wing, she saw several shadowy figures moving out from the trees and running across the meadow to extinguish the beacons.

Understandably, the FAB operatives were anxious to remove all trace of the secret runway before it was spotted by French aerial reconnaissance.

Arabella slid the cockpit canopy shut and jumped to the ground. She was of medium height, with long chestnut hair that emerged from beneath her leather flying cap and flowed over her shoulders. She wore a cream scarf and a loose white shirt under her double-breasted leather jacket. Her baggy black trousers were tucked into knee-length leather boots. The jacket had been her father's and was a favourite of hers. Its rich brown leather, ornamented with brass buttons, belts and buckles, seemed to belong to a more heroic age.

From a panel in the side of the fuselage she hauled out a large, brass-studded leather trunk. Staggering a little under its weight, she manhandled it to the ground. She was about to open it when a noise behind her made her turn. A portly man in a beret and a grubby coat was approaching her across the field. She didn't recognise him, and wondered what had happened to Bernard, her usual contact.

'*Bonsoir, mademoiselle,*' he wheezed as he approached. 'You are late.' He examined her with small, squinty eyes and a twitching, nervous smile. His nose was squashed almost flat against his face, giving his voice a nasal, squeaky tone.

'I ran into some trouble over Paris,' explained Arabella. 'Two warcraft from the Imperial Fleet. Where is Ber–?'

21

'It is getting harder these days,' the Frenchman interrupted. 'The skies are getting busier. Were you followed?'

She shook her head. 'What happened to Bernard?'

'Bernard is dead,' said the man with a shrug. 'Killed last night by Guizot's thugs.'

Arabella knew of Marshal Guizot, the ruthless head of Napoleon's secret police. She had not known Bernard well, but he had seemed a nice, gentle sort, perhaps not really cut out for the life of a spy. His death was a reminder of the daily danger they all faced.

'I am Gaston, his replacement,' the man added.

'Well, monsieur,' said Arabella, as she unsnapped the lock of the trunk and raised the lid, 'I'm here now. So perhaps you can tell me the purpose of this mission?'

The Frenchman didn't reply. He was too busy staring at the thing lying in Arabella's trunk.

She hauled it out, straightened it and set it on its feet. The object resembled a small man, about three feet in height. He was dressed in a miniature frock coat, cravat, breeches and top hat. His gleaming metal face wore a blank expression. His glassy eyes, with their black centres, stared intently at nothing.

Arabella pressed an ignition switch at the back of the automaton, and a low, rhythmic popping sound started up in his chest as a gas-fired engine came to life. A soft yellow light swam into his eyes, and they became less glassy, more animated, their black centres beginning to rove around. A plume of exhaust gas hissed from a tiny pipe in the top of the man's hat. Then came a chorus of muted squeaks as the joints in his shoulders, elbows, hips and knees began to flex.

'*Qu'est-ce que c'est?*' Gaston breathed.

'This is Miles,' answered Arabella. 'Did you have a good flight, Miles?'

There was a slight whirring sound, before a calm voice replied: 'No, my lady, it cannot be said that I had a good flight, since I was not in any functional sense alive at the time.'

The mouth did not move as he spoke. The voice, which seemed to come from inside the brass head, had a weary, resigned sort of tone, as if he'd long ago learned to tolerate the stupidity of humans.

'*Mon Dieu!*' said Gaston. 'What will you English come up with next?'

Arabella explained. 'He's a Mobile Independent Logical Englishman Simulacrum – Miles for short. The first and, so far, the only one of his kind. An experiment, you might say. They asked me to give him a try-out. This is his first mission.'

'What can he do?' the Frenchman asked, eyeing Miles warily.

'We're not exactly sure yet,' Arabella admitted. 'The technicians who imagineered him are hoping I'll find out and tell them.' She looked around her. The field was now dark, all the beacons extinguished. 'So, what am I here for?' she asked.

With an effort, Gaston turned his gaze away from the mechanical man. 'I have had a meeting with Agent Z,' he said.

Arabella was impressed. Agent Z was a legend in espionage circles. In the last three years he had given the British much valuable information, including details of the planned French invasion. She suspected he must be someone quite senior within the French military, to have access to such top-quality intelligence. But Agent Z always took care to speak through at least two layers of intermediaries. No one she knew had ever met him.

'You mean *the* Agent Z?'

'*Mais oui,*' frowned Gaston. 'How many can there be?'

At this point, Miles piped up: 'May I remind you, my lady, that Agent Z is not believed to operate in this way. It is not his habit to pass information directly to low-ranking field operatives. Are you really going to trust this man, whom you have never met before?'

Gaston looked down at Miles as if the automaton were a cowpat he'd just trodden in. 'What can this… this piece of junk possibly know? "Low-ranking field operative" indeed! He has no right to speak of me in this way.'

Arabella thought for a moment – Miles had a point. 'Do you have any proof of who you are?' she asked.

'I am here, am I not?' replied Gaston in a surly tone. 'As arranged with your people in London. Of course

I don't carry documentation with me – suppose I got caught? I may be only a "low-ranking field operative", but I'm not stupid.'

'Who is your unit's contact in London?'

'He calls himself the Steel Duke.'

Arabella nodded. That was the code name of Sir George Jarrett, Britain's spymaster-in-chief.

'I wasn't told to expect you.'

'As I say, Bernard died only last night. There was no time to warn your people of the change.'

She decided she had no choice but to trust him.

'So that's what this is about, then?' she said. 'You're here to pass on a message from Agent Z?'

Gaston nodded. 'He says the invasion will be arriving on a broad front, extending from Dorset to Kent. It is planned for September.'

Arabella nodded. This confirmed reports she'd heard from other sources. It was good information. But she was puzzled, and starting to feel angry.

'Why did you not just send us this information in an encrypted aetherwave message? I risked life and limb getting here!'

'Calm down, mademoiselle,' tutted Gaston. 'There is something else. Something I have to show you. You must come with me, in my steam carriage. It is not far.'

'I should warn you, my lady,' said Miles, 'that I am very uneasy about the suggestion that we should go for a ride in this gentleman's steam carriage. I have input the facts of our present situation and performed some calculations based on probabilities, and I have concluded that this is ninety per cent likely to be a trap.'

'Well, you need not worry, Mr Metal Man, because you are not invited!' snarled Gaston. He looked as if he was about to kick Miles.

'Miles comes with us,' said Arabella emphatically, stepping between Gaston and the Logical Englishman. Turning to Miles, she murmured: 'I don't think we have any choice. There's no one else here to meet us. If we don't go with him, the whole mission will have been pointless.'

'That may be true, my lady, but –'

'But nothing! Now come along. Monsieur, lead us to your carriage.'

CHAPTER THREE

THE
FORMULA

They followed Gaston back across the meadow towards the woods. Miles moved jerkily across the bumpy ground as he strove to keep up with Arabella. The bubbling of his little engine grew louder with the effort, as did the hiss of the waste gases pouring out of the top of his hat.

Gaston's vehicle was parked off a dirt track a little way into the woods. It was a boat-shaped carriage of wood and brass, with big fat wheels and lots of exposed pipework sprouting through the bonnet like the tentacles of some chrome-plated monster.

Gaston opened the brass-bound wooden trunk at the back of the vehicle. 'That thing can go in here,' he said, indicating Miles.

Arabella shook her head. 'No, he rides in the carriage with me, or I'm not coming.'

She wasn't sure why she wanted Miles with her. She had no idea what he was for. But neither did Gaston, and she liked the fact that the Frenchman was scared of him. It balanced things out a little. She was taking a risk by getting into this carriage, and now he was being forced to take a risk, too.

Gaston shrugged bitterly and held open the rear door for both of them to climb in.

After a half-hour drive along country lanes in Gaston's clanking, snorting steam carriage, they stopped opposite a small turn-off on the left, obstructed by a wrought-iron gate set in a high brick wall. It looked like the entrance to a stately home.

'Where are we?' asked Arabella.

'The Laboratoire de la Révolution,' replied Gaston. He pointed up the driveway towards the dim silhouette of a building. 'In there,' he said, 'is the formula for the most powerful weapon in the world: the weapon that could win the war for France. In fact, it could win any war. Armed with that weapon, there is nothing to stop Napoléon from becoming master of the world.'

Arabella shuddered. 'What kind of weapon are you talking about?'

'The Aetheric Shield,' answered Gaston in an almost

reverent tone. 'Invisible armour. A warcraft dressed in the Aetheric Shield will be invulnerable to any bomb, shell or bullet yet devised. *Titan* will be dressed in the Aetheric Shield.'

'*Titan*,' gasped Arabella. 'You mean the vessel that will spearhead the invasion?'

'*Exactement!* It will be unstoppable.'

'We can't let that happen!'

'*Je suis d'accord.* Which is why you must steal the formula for this monstrous weapon, mademoiselle.'

Arabella stared at him. 'I –'

'*Mais oui.* That is why we have brought you here. So you can steal the formula and take it back to your superiors in Britain. Then *your* scientists can create their own Aetheric Shield. Or, better, develop a bomb that can penetrate it.'

'You want me to go in there and steal the formula?'

A smile spread across Gaston's wide face. 'We have heard of your skills at breaking and entering, mademoiselle.'

'I don't have any such skills!' cried Arabella. 'I think you may have got me mixed up with someone else.'

Gaston stared at her, shocked. 'But you are Béatrice, *n'est-ce pas?*'

'I am Arabella.'

'But we asked for Béatrice!' Gaston thumped the steering wheel in frustration.

Beatrice Darlow was a fellow member of the Sky

Sisters, the top-secret corps of aerial spies that Arabella was part of. There were five of them, each chosen for a particular skill. Arabella's was flying; Beatrice's was breaking and entering. As a child, Beatrice had been a highly successful thief, before being recruited by Emmeline Stuart, who was Arabella's aunt and the leader of the Sky Sisters.

'Someone must have got their wires crossed,' said Arabella despairingly.

'I may be able to help, my lady,' said Miles. 'I possess some algorithms for lock-picking.'

Gaston threw up his hands in exasperation. '*Eh bien!* So this mission of so many weeks' planning, with so many lives put at risk, is to be entrusted to a girl with no experience and her friend made out of tin! *Maintenant j'ai tout vu!* Now I have seen it all.'

This was too much for Arabella's pride. 'We will do this, monsieur! Just tell me where the formula is located, and we shall steal it.'

Shaking his head and muttering, Gaston reached into the pocket of his shabby coat and pulled out a crinkled piece of paper, which he handed to Arabella. Drawn in black ink on the paper was the floor layout of a building, showing walls, doors, windows and other fixtures. 'This is the plan of the ground floor of the *laboratoire*,' explained Gaston. 'The formula is to be found in a cabinet in this room here.' He pointed to a small room, marked with a cross, off a long corridor.

'What about security?' Arabella asked.

'Of course, the laboratoire has many guards,' said Gaston. 'But fear not, I have a diversion planned for them. I have laid an explosive charge on one side of the building, timed to go off at midnight, which is in...' – he fished out a grimy silver timepiece from his pocket – '...just over six minutes. That will send them all scurrying towards the west wing of the house, giving you time to break in through the front entrance and steal the formula.'

He made it all sound so straightforward, but Arabella wasn't convinced. 'What if this diversion doesn't work?'

'Then you will have to deal with the guards some other way.'

'Easy for you to say,' she snorted. 'How many locks will we have to break open?'

'One at the front entrance, one to get into the room, and one to get into the cabinet. If you can open these, steal the formula and get away before the guards return, then *voilà!* – the job is done.'

Arabella stuffed the plan into the pocket of her flying jacket. She kept her hand there, waiting for it to stop shaking. It was one thing facing down giant warcraft in her natural element, the sky. Down here on the ground, she felt far less sure of herself – a child in an adult world. Gaston made it seem so easy. But he must know these guards would shoot on sight. Normally, her work was about liaison – making contacts with local nationalists and anti-Bonapartists, and getting information from them. Occasionally, she took part in acts of sabotage. Never until now had she been asked to confront armed guards alone. But she couldn't back out – it simply wasn't in her nature. She opened the carriage door and stepped into the road. Miles jumped out after her.

'*Bonne chance!*' smirked Gaston.

She didn't like the expression on the Frenchman's face. It made her think of the other possibility – that this was a trap.

The storm had cleared, and the night was calm and mild. Even so, Arabella felt a chill as she approached the gated driveway. At least she had Miles with her. The little metal man by her side, despite his puffing and creaking and his odd way of moving, was a reassuring presence. He seemed to know what he was doing.

She watched and waited in the shadows near the gate. A couple of guards dressed in pale green uniforms came into view, strolling towards them up the driveway. The guards stopped at the gate, muttering to each other in low voices, before turning and making their way slowly back towards the house. 'Get a move on!' Arabella silently urged them. She and Miles had to get within sprinting distance of the house before the diversionary explosion, or the whole plan would fail. She checked her wristwatch – a chunky leather and brass ornament with exposed cogs. Midnight was less than four minutes away.

When she was sure the guards were out of earshot,

she began climbing up the gate. At the top, she glanced down and was disappointed to see that Miles hadn't moved. 'Come on!' she hissed.

'My lady,' he puffed unhappily, 'I'm afraid I lack a facility for ascending portals such as this...'

Arabella gave a sigh and swiftly returned to the ground. She grasped him by the shoulders and picked him up. Absurdly, she worried how this might affect his dignity.

'I hope you don't mind?'

'It's quite all right, my lady,' he said.

Taking a firm hold of the Logical Englishman with one arm, she unsteadily remounted the gate. It was hard going, but luckily he wasn't too heavy and by bracing herself against the gate she was able to lift him. When they reached the top, she took a deep breath and heaved him over to the other side. There followed some awkward manoeuvring during which, at one stage, she had to use her cheek for support and dearly wished she had a third hand. Eventually, they reached the driveway on the other side of the gate. Arabella quickly led Miles beneath the cover of some trees by the side of the driveway. According to her watch there was just over a minute to go.

They edged their way through the trees towards the building, an imposing brick structure with dark, narrow windows and steeply sloping roofs. The closer they got, the more uneasy Arabella began to feel. The mission didn't make sense. If FAB had managed to get hold of a floor plan, and even planted an explosive device in the grounds, why couldn't they also have stolen the plans? Why bring an English agent all the way over here to do this one thing? By now, she was almost certain she was being led into a trap. She looked around fearfully, imagining French Imperial agents lurking behind every tree. She wondered what calculations were flickering through Miles's head right now.

'Do you still think this is a trap?' she whispered to him.

'I suspect so, my lady. I further suspect that it is too late for us to do much about it. Any attempt to flee now is bound to fail, and may even result in our deaths.'

'What a cheery companion you are!' said Arabella with a shiver.

They had reached the edge of the trees. Here, the driveway opened up into a large, D-shaped forecourt. Beyond lay the laboratory building. She could see six guards stationed at various points around its perimeter. They carried long rifles, with bayonets, on their shoulders. Gas lighting illuminated the brick walls, but there was no light emanating from the windows – she hoped this meant there would be nobody inside. She took a final look at her watch. The seconds ticked their way towards twelve o'clock. Ten... nine... eight... seven... – 'Get ready to run, Miles,' she whispered – ... four... three... two... one...

CHAPTER FOUR

THE
LABORATOIRE

Silence... Had Gaston lied about the explosion? Then he must have lied about everything else! So this was a trap!

'We should get out of here,' Arabella whispered urgently to Miles.

She never heard his reply.

A massive *ka-boom* tore through the still night air like the slam of a giant's fist. Arabella was momentarily rocked backwards by a wave of heat. When she reopened her eyes she saw smoke billowing out of the west wing. The source of the explosion was hidden from view, around a corner, some fifty yards from the front entrance. The guards were running about, eyes wide with panic. One of them gave a shout, and the other five followed him towards the smoke. Three more guards emerged from the trees and they, too, converged on the stricken west wing.

This was Arabella's chance.

'Quick!' she cried to Miles, and she raced across the forecourt towards the porticoed entrance. This, she knew, was the most dangerous moment. If any of the guards happened to glance back, they would see her clearly in the gaslight. Miles clanked after her as fast as he could. He had just joined her in the sanctuary of the entrance when they heard a nearby shout and footsteps approaching across the gravel. Arabella fled behind one of the two thick pillars of the portico, hauling Miles close to her.

The footsteps slowed to walking pace, then stopped. In the background they could hear the shouts and cries of the other guards. *'Qui est–ce?'* came a gruff voice, very close by. *'Pierre, est-ce toi?'* The guard was on the far side of the pillar, just a few feet from her. Arabella heard him moving slowly beneath the portico, and she began edging around the pillar in the other direction to keep out of his sight. He stopped again and, without meaning to, Arabella found herself right behind him, just inches from his hairy neck. At any moment he would see her or Miles. She had to act!

Moving as swiftly and silently as she could, she reached into her shoulder bag and took out the brass syringe she always carried there. It was filled with chloral hydrate – Emmeline had given it to her to knock herself out in the event of capture by the enemy.

('They'll think you're dead, my dear – and hopefully they'll leave you alone.')

Arabella removed the protective cap. She couldn't control her breathing, which sounded like the roar of a cyclone in her ears. There was a faint bluish line beneath the skin on the side of the guard's neck – a vein. She pushed her fingers through the two brass rings of the syringe and laid her thumb on the plunger.

She heard Emmeline's calm voice in her head: 'Just do it, Arabella.'

Then she threw her left arm around the man's neck and pulled it as tight as she could.

He gasped, then choked, as his body writhed and his hands began grabbing at her arm. His neck was twisting this way and that, but she located her mark and drove the needle in as hard as she could. Within seconds he was slumped, as docile as a sleeping baby. Hurriedly, she dragged him into the bushes that grew at the base of the wall next to the entrance, masking him from sight.

'Fine work, my lady,' commented Miles as he eyed the unconscious guard. 'There are at least eight others, though, and this incident has delayed us. I calculate that we now have almost no chance of completing our mission before they return here to apprehend us.'

His makers probably didn't intend Miles as a morale-booster, reflected Arabella, but could they not have made him just a little less pessimistic about everything? It was becoming quite dispiriting.

While Arabella kept watch, Miles went to work. He pointed the jointed brass index finger of his right hand at the door, and a thin, key-like metal tube emerged from his fingertip and entered the lock. Gently, he twisted his hand left and right as if feeling for something inside.

From the west wing of the house, Arabella could hear a faint crackle of flames. Sparks danced in the air amid the smoke. This was more than a diversion – Gaston had started a fire. Good! Whatever Miles said, that should keep the guards occupied for a while.

She flinched at a sound from above her – a dull metallic squeak. A weathervane, perhaps, or a loose drainpipe moving in the night breeze. Or was it the squeak of a crossbow being tightened?

She moved further under the portico, out of range of any rooftop crossbowmen, and concentrated instead on the soft little clicks being made by Miles's finger-key as it explored the inner workings of the lock. She wished he would hurry up.

At last the door swung open. They were in!

'Good show, Miles,' cried Arabella as they slipped inside the building.

At the far end of the hallway lay a long corridor spanning the building's entire width. Arabella hid in the shadows at the corner and glanced one way, then the other: the corridor seemed empty. According to the plan, they had to turn right here. The corridor was lined with French Revolution-era paintings.

Here and there, against the wood-panelled walls, they passed glass cases displaying pieces of lab equipment – beakers, burners, tubes and bulbs, cranks and clockwork mechanisms crammed with dials, springs and levers. On a pedestal, they came across the metal head of an automaton. The glass-topped skull revealed all the intricate cogs, gears and switches of its brain. Miles stopped in his tracks when he saw this. A worried spurt of steam puffed from his hat.

Arabella put a hand on his shoulder. 'Don't worry,' she said. 'I'm sure that won't happen to you.'

'I do not worry for myself, my lady, only for Britain. If the Bonapartists are also developing automata, then the threat is even worse than I feared. Imagine, if you will, an army of them, protected by the Aetheric Shield, advancing through our countryside.'

'All the more reason not to get caught,' said Arabella. 'I'm sure they could learn a lot by taking you apart, piece by piece...'

They stopped in front of a door about halfway down the right-hand side of the corridor. According to the plan, this led to the room containing the formula.

While Miles went to work on the lock, Arabella kept lookout. The guards would be on high alert – they might even have guessed by now that the explosion was a diversion. She braced herself for the sound of footsteps.

It didn't take Miles more than a minute to pick the lock. But on entering the room, Arabella's heart sank.

The walls of the small, windowless chamber were lined with polished oak drawers. There were about thirty of them, and none were labelled. It would take at least an hour to unlock and search each of them for the formula – yet they probably had no more than a few minutes before this place was swarming with guards.

Miles had already turned his attention to the lock on the first drawer. In less than a minute, he'd broken into it. Arabella heaved the drawer open. It extended much further than she expected. More than five feet of files stretched out before her. 'It'll be like searching for a needle in a haystack,' she said with a groan, as she got down on her knees and began riffling through the files. Meanwhile, the automaton went to work opening the next drawer along.

Suddenly the corridor outside was filled with Gallic shouts and cries and running footsteps. Arabella frantically cast about for somewhere to hide, but, apart from the drawers, the room was perfectly empty.

'May I suggest your ladyship secretes herself in here?' said Miles, indicating the open drawer of the filing cabinet.

Arabella stared at the long drawer and realised it was a perfect fit for her, if she could only squeeze herself beneath all those hanging files. 'What about you?' she asked the automaton.

'Do not concern yourself about that,' he replied, pushing aside some files so she could step in. As the shouts and booted footsteps grew louder, she sat down in the drawer and slid her legs beneath the files, then wriggled the rest of herself in. The edges of the files dug uncomfortably into her body and pressed against her face, and she had to bend her legs awkwardly to make space for them. Miles gave the drawer a push, there was a whistle of sliding metal rails and she found herself locked away in absolute darkness. It was stifling and airless and she almost choked on the dry, ancient, papery smell. She could hear the dull thump of her heart, and the stampeding of guards outside. Surely they'd seen Miles by now! It wouldn't take them long to find her. The volume of their yells and the cocking of their rifles told her they were inside the room – but there was no sound of drawers being opened.

Gradually, the noise of the guards faded and silence fell once more. Now a new fear overcame Arabella. If the guards had gone, taking Miles prisoner, she would be left in here to die of suffocation! Desperately, she pushed against the back wall with her feet – but it was the back wall of the drawer, not the room, and no amount of pushing could help. She thrust her arms up through the files and pressed her fingers against the underside of the drawer above, but lacked the leverage to force her own drawer open. She felt herself becoming breathless with panic. Her lungs struggled for air. There was no hope of rescue – she had to face that. The drawer would soon become her coffin!

Arabella had almost resigned herself to this bizarre and undignified death when there came a squeak and a tug, and light and air filtered into her black world. 'My lady,' said a contrite-looking Miles, 'I humbly apologise for leaving you for so long in a compartment of such restricted dimensions.'

'It's quite all right,' gasped Arabella, hurriedly squeezing herself out of the drawer.

'It must have been most unpleasant for your ladyship,' continued Miles. 'However, I was obliged to wait until the guards had departed the building.'

'How on earth did you manage to evade them, Miles?'

'I posed as an exhibit, my lady.'

'An exhibit?'

Miles demonstrated by falling very still. All traces of steam disappeared from his hat funnel. He even dowsed the yellow light from his eyes. He became, to all appearances, lifeless. 'I hoped they might consider me a companion piece for the automaton head in the corridor,' he added, after stirring back to life. 'To my astonishment, they did.'

'Hiding in plain sight! Miles, that's ingenious!'

The automaton made a small bow.

'Now, we must find that formula before they come back,' said Arabella, stooping to examine the files in the drawer that had so nearly become her tomb. She quickly discovered that the files had been placed in alphabetical order. That made things a lot easier! This was the 'A' drawer. But what was the French for 'Aetheric Shield'? She wracked her brains.

Miles had meanwhile gone back to work on the lock of the second drawer. As the 'B' drawer slid open, she suddenly remembered: the French for shield was *bouclier*. And there, right in the middle of the Bs, she found it: *Bouclier Etherique* – the Aetheric Shield. She pulled out the heavy grey folder and started flicking through it. It was full of papers dense with complex equations and diagrams.

'Eureka!' Arabella whispered. 'You can stop opening drawers now, Miles. I've found it!'

The Logical Englishman withdrew his finger-key from the next lock and turned to her. 'Congratulations, my lady. Although I fear it will all be to no avail, for we will soon be caught.'

'Nonsense!' said Arabella, tiring of her companion's relentless pessimism. 'We've done the hard part. Now all we have to do is find a way out of here!' She placed the folder in her shoulder bag. 'Let's take this back to Gaston and show him what a girl with no experience and her friend made of tin are capable of.'

'Brass,' corrected Miles a little sniffily. 'Brass is an alloy of copper and zinc. It contains no tin.'

They were moving back along the corridor when Arabella heard a sound. It came from the hallway up ahead – a barely audible rasping sound, like the scrape of a boot on carpet or the whisper of a coat brushing against furniture. She stopped still, heart thumping. Motioning Miles to press himself flat against the wall, she ducked behind one of the display cabinets.

The only illumination in the corridor was the moonlight that filtered through the windows. It washed the paintings and the scientific exhibits with a chill, grey light. The hallway was in complete shadow. She glanced at Miles, who was once again doing his admirable impression of an inanimate museum exhibit.

Arabella listened hard for another minute, but could hear nothing further. Was someone was lying in wait for them at the end of the corridor? The guards were nowhere in sight, but their suspicions must have been aroused. Almost certainly, one or more would be lying in wait up ahead. How would they react when they found the incriminating file in her hands? Most likely they would take her before Marshal Guizot, and his torturers would go to work on her. Gaston would probably be there, too, his podgy face creased with amusement as he enjoyed the success of his clever little deception. He had probably murdered Bernard himself. Oh, she had been a fool to be so taken in! But she would make amends by being brave. Let the torturers do their worst, she would tell them nothing!

'Miles,' she whispered into the darkness, 'what do you suggest we do?'

'There may be a back entrance, my lady. It is our one remaining hope.'

'How do you rate our chances?'

'Less than one per cent.'

She chuckled bitterly. 'Well, I suppose that's better than nothing!'

CHAPTER FIVE

THE SHAPE IN THE DARK

rabella examined the plan, and soon found what she was looking for. She signalled to Miles to follow, then began creeping eastwards along the corridor, away from the hallway. They moved slowly, keeping to the shadows. Finally they came to a wider area with bare white walls and a tiled floor. To their right lay a staircase; to their left, as marked on the plan, was a door leading to the grounds at the back of the house. Arabella moved to the door, wiped the sweat from her palm and carefully turned the handle. Fortunately it didn't squeak. The door was unlocked. Cool night air, smelling of damp grass and leaves, gusted into the room. It felt good on her skin. The grounds were shadowy with bushes and trees. A mist had descended, making everything indistinct. Anyone could be hiding out there – she'd never know until it was too late.

'Come on,' she whispered to Miles, and out they went. At the bottom of a set of steps, she turned right, hoping to find a path that would lead them to the front of the building. A rustling made her stop. Coming towards her out of the blue mist was the head of a goat!

It had long ears and tapering horns, and swayed like a snake demon, blocking her path. She froze, hardly daring to believe what she was seeing. Then a breeze blew the goat's head apart, and she saw it was nothing more than a cluster of leaves. The horns were long, thin branches.

She breathed deeply, trying to calm the hammering in her chest. *There's no one here*, she told herself firmly. *I've been infected by Miles's gloominess. The guards are back at their stations. The noise in the hallway was probably just a mouse. Gaston will be waiting for us in his steam carriage, and in half an hour I shall be airborne again, taking with me the vital plans for the Aetheric Shield.*

Arabella walked purposefully across a patch of damp grass towards a path that ran along the eastern side of the house. The gate leading to the path stood invitingly open.

A trap? No, just very poor security!

She pulled open the gate – and nearly died of fright. Standing less than ten yards away was a tall, slim shape. It was hard to tell what it was, with the moon behind it. But a long, narrow gleam by its waist told her that the shape was carrying a weapon, and it was pointed at her.

She began to back away.

'Don't move!' barked the shape. It sounded like a young man. Surprisingly, it had an American accent. The USA was an ally of Britain, or was supposed to be. Many Americans, she knew, felt a sentimental attachment to Napoleon. Some had even joined up to fight for the Bonapartists. This one sounded young – maybe even younger than her. Hopefully, he would scare easily.

'I must warn you,' she said. 'I have a highly dangerous automaton with me. If you don't let me pass, I shall be forced to give him the order to kill you.'

The young man came closer. As his features emerged into view, she was disturbed to see that he was grinning. Even more troubling than his smile were his eyes, which were dark, and distractingly beautiful.

'You mean Miles?' he chuckled, peering behind her at the mechanical man at her heels. 'You wouldn't hurt a fly, now would you, Miles?' His eyes flickered back to Arabella and he studied her carefully, seeming to examine every contour of her cheeks, every eyelash. She felt herself going pink, and looked away to disguise her discomfort. How did he know Miles's name? He didn't seem to act like a security guard. Neither was he dressed like one, in his dirty, double-breasted military jacket with brass buttons, open at the top, displaying a casually knotted neck scarf. He seemed more like…

…like someone in her own line of work!

'What do you want?' she asked finally.

The boy scratched his chin with the long barrel of his ornately decorated revolver. 'What I want is the folder in your bag. I'm most obliged to you, and to Miles, for breaking into this place and stealing it for me.'

So the boy wasn't trying to stop her from stealing the formula – he wanted it for himself!

An idea suddenly struck her.

'You're working for the Americans!' she blurted. 'You're planning to hand this over to your bosses in Washington. Admit it!'

The boy frowned and shook his head – he almost looked offended. 'I don't work for the Americans, the French, the Russians or anyone else,' he said. 'I work for myself.'

'So you're a mercenary!' she said, disgusted by the thought – she had never understood how anyone could fight a war motivated only by money. 'Who's paying you to steal the formula?'

'No one. Like I say, I work for myself.' He nodded towards her bag. 'I'm planning on selling it to the highest bidder, and if the rumours about the shield are true, it should bag me a pretty penny.' He pointed the gun at her, his smile now fading. 'Hand it over, Lady Arabella, if you value your life.'

She started at the sound of her name. 'How do you know who I am?'

'My good friend Gaston filled me in,' smirked the boy.

Arabella ground her teeth. *That double-crossing, two-faced scoundrel...!* She would have dearly loved to wipe the smiles off both their faces. 'None of this will make a jot of difference,' she said defiantly. 'The British will get the Aetheric Shield, you mark my words.'

'Oh, I'm hoping so,' said the boy. 'And I hope they pay me top dollar for it!'

She briefly considered making a run for it, but quickly dismissed the idea. There was a ruthlessness lurking behind the boy's playful smile. She had no doubt he would kill her before she could get two paces. Reluctantly, she took the folder out of her shoulder bag and handed it over to him.

'Thank you, ma'am,' he said, giving a brief bow. 'You've been most co-operative. The name's Ben, by the way. Ben Forrester.' He said it cheerily, as if she were his new best friend. 'It's been mighty fine doing business with you.' He began retreating up the path, keeping the gun trained on her all the while. 'Who knows, maybe our paths will cross again some day.'

He disappeared through a gap in the trees that lined the path. After hearing him scamper away, Arabella chased after him. She could barely make out the path he'd followed through the thick woods that lay on this side of the property. Branches tore at her clothes, and roots threatened to trip her up as she ran. Finally, she came to the high brick wall that surrounded the grounds. A rope ladder dangled from its crest. From the other side of the wall she could hear the clank, snort and screech of Gaston's steam carriage. She clambered up the ladder and was in time to witness the carriage disappearing around a bend in the road. Her little metal companion arrived soon afterwards, puffing and burbling. Three minutes later, she had helped him over the wall and they both stood on the grassy verge of the empty road.

'Oh, Miles,' Arabella said. 'I'm afraid we've been used quite dreadfully by those two appalling men.'

'I'm very sorry, my lady.'

Arabella looked down at the diminutive Logical Englishman standing forlornly at her side. 'I thought you might have a trick or two up your sleeve,' she sighed. 'Like a gun, for example.'

'I'm afraid my strengths do not lie in that direction.'

'Never mind,' she shrugged. 'You win some, you lose some. Now, how far is it to the airfield?'

'Twelve and a quarter miles, my lady.'

'Well then, we'd best start walking, hadn't we?'

PART II

16 JULY 1845

"Strange-lookin' cloud. Big and round, like a giant puffball, not movin' nor changin' shape, as clouds normally do. The wind were blowin', but that cloud, it stayed still as stone."

Taranis

FILED
REFERENCE NO
280756

Smoke from
main engine

"It looked like some
sort of... bird, big as one
o' them prehistoric beasts
or maybe even bigger.
'Its wings were wider
and broader than our
entire vessel, and when
they stretched to their
full extent, they cast a
shadow deep as night over
all of us.

"This
fearsome
sharp beak that
opened, showin' a tongue
that seemed to drip with fire.
It had talons bigger than elephant
tusks, which it plunged into the fabric of our
vessel. The thing had us secure as a newborn
lamb in the jaws of a lion."

BRITISH IMPERIAL
SECRET SERVICE

Restricted
☒ Confidential
☐ Mission
☐ Publication

CONFIDENTIAL

Dread Eagle

Wing movement is powered by a water-tube boiler: hundreds of steel tubes heated by a large coal furnace. Coal is stored in great bunkers inside the chest and fed down long chutes to a conveyor belt that continuously stokes the furnace.

Cold water is forced into the boiler by injectors. High-pressure steam generates energy for the wing motion in flight mode. Exhaust steam escapes by way of conical hoods.

The claws are powered by the reactive turbine, using the forward velocity of the steam to generate kinetic energy to drive the wheels.

Front elevation

Human for scale

Air leaks damage efficiency. An extractor pump sucks out excess air from the mechanism.

Human for scale

Side elevation

CONF

SURVEILLANCE

FILED
REFERENCE NO
2807?6
BRITISH IMPERIAL
SECRET SERVICE

Restricted
☒ Confidential
☐ Mission
☐ ????

CHAPTER SIX

THE SKY SISTERS

Arabella stood on the promenade at Brighton and stared at the empty beach. Instead of bathing huts, colourful parasols and laughing children, all she could see was endless rolls of barbed wire, held in place by rows of wooden posts, stretching in either direction as far as the eye could see.

Each week brought fresh rumours of a French invasion, and of course Britain had to be prepared. The barbed wire was a necessary part of her coastal defences. All the same, it was a dismaying sight. Arabella had happy memories of childhood holidays down here in Brighton – eating candyfloss, watching Punch and Judy shows, riding the carousel. She would go down with her nanny, and sometimes, when he wasn't on a mission, Father would come, too. On a warm, sunny day like today, people ought to be down on the beach, playing and swimming…

'Don't look so sad, Bella,' said Cassie, who was standing next to her. 'One day, this war will be over.'

Cassie Ray was one of the Sky Sisters. Tall and strong, her special skill was martial arts – though you wouldn't know it, dressed as she was now in her white bonnet, blue skirt and matching riding habit. Arabella was in similar attire, though her skirt and riding habit were burgundy red. Arabella much preferred her flying outfit to these high-necked, tight-waisted jackets and wide skirts, but she understood the need to dress conventionally when off duty. Emmeline was always reminding the Sky Sisters not to draw attention to themselves.

'I could have helped to end it sooner,' Arabella sighed, 'if only I'd managed to bring home that formula.'

Cassie gave her shoulder a reassuring squeeze. 'You did the best you could,' she said. 'How could you possibly have known it was a set-up?' Cassie might be strong, but she was also sweet and sensitive – perhaps Arabella's only true friend.

'Emmeline didn't see it that way,' said Arabella, biting her lip at the memory of that humiliating debriefing session with her aunt on her return to London. 'She said I should never have trusted the

Frenchman, Gaston. As soon as Bernard didn't show, I should have high-tailed it out of there.'

'But think of all the extra intelligence you managed to gather,' Cassie pointed out.

Dear, sweet Cassie – always determined to see the bright side of everything! Arabella sometimes wondered how she'd get on with Miles.

'We'd never have known about the Aetheric Shield if you'd just upped and left.'

'Yes, and a fat lot of good it's done us *knowing* about it,' commented Arabella. 'Everyone's in a tizzy about this shield, but without the formula we've no idea what it is or how it works.'

'We've got our top agents on the case, though, haven't we?' said Cassie. 'They're scouring the world for this mysterious American. I'm sure they'll find him sooner or later.'

'Ugh, don't talk to me about that frightful young man,' snapped Arabella, surprising herself with how angry she felt at the very mention of him. 'I hope he disappears into whatever squalid hole he came out of and never shows his face again. People like Mr Forrester make me sick, they really do. They believe in nothing except money, and war is simply an opportunity to get rich.'

'Methinks the lady doth protest too much!' came a soft, girlish voice from behind them.

They turned to see Diana standing there, holding three ice cream cones. Diana Temple was the fifth of the Sky Sisters – an expert finder, who sometimes carried her talent into her personal life.

'What are you talking about?' asked Arabella, taking one of the ice creams.

'I caught a peek at the minutes from your debriefing session,' Diana confessed with a smirk. 'I couldn't help noticing your description of young Mr Forrester's eyes as "dark, and rather intense"!'

Cassie laughed loudly, and Arabella coloured. 'That information is strictly classified,' she said.

'I know, dear,' giggled Diana. 'But I hardly think the intensity of a boy's eyes is likely to represent a threat to national security – unless he uses them for malicious purposes, like distracting a girl while she's supposed to be spying for Britain!'

'I wasn't distracted!'

Arabella had always thought Diana the most beautiful of the Sky Sisters. She also found her the hardest to trust. Maybe she was just too good at her job. As spies, they had all been trained in the arts of guile and deceit, but some – it had to be said – were better at this than others, and Diana was a natural.

'Where are Emmeline and Beatrice?' asked Cassie, tactfully changing the subject.

'Last time I saw Emmeline, she was using her aethercell,' said Diana, after taking a lick of her ice cream. 'She was checking with Shoreham airbase to see if we can go up this afternoon. Apparently there's a storm brewing. As for Beatrice, I've no idea. She's probably on the Queen's Road pickpocketing the tourists as they emerge from the station.'

This was, of course, grossly unfair – Beatrice had ceased her criminal ways long ago – yet so typical of Diana that the others didn't even bother to be offended on their colleague's behalf.

The girl herself turned up a moment later. Beatrice Darlow was small and unremarkable, with dull brown hair. When Arabella first met her, she made no impression at all. In fact, Beatrice had the perfect look for a petty thief-turned-spy – in the drab dresses she liked to wear, she was hard to spot in a crowd, and she had the kind of face that eyewitnesses always struggled to remember. As usual, it took her fellow Sky Sisters a while to realise she was there at all.

'Ahem,' coughed Beatrice. They all turned. She was holding up the latest edition of the *Daily Proclaimer*. The headline read:

ANOTHER AIRSHIP DISAPPEARS OVER ATLANTIC

'That's the third this month!' cried Arabella, grabbing the paper and scanning the article for details.

'Who could be doing this?' Cassie wondered.

'No one has any idea,' said Beatrice.

'It's the same story each time,' murmured Arabella as she read the article. 'No trace of wreckage, no survivors. It just disappeared into thin air. A hundred and forty-one passengers and crew – British holidaymakers mostly, heading for New York. All gone!'

'Do you think the French are behind it?' asked Beatrice.

'The last airship that disappeared was a French transporter,' Diana pointed out. 'I hardly think they'd be targeting their own craft. No, I don't think this has anything to do with the war. It's something completely new.'

A chill wind blew in from the east. Arabella drew her shawl more tightly around her shoulders. On the horizon, above the Chain Pier, dark clouds were mustering.

'This isn't good news for Operation Zeus,' murmured Beatrice.

'What's Operation Zeus?' asked Cassie.

'Haven't you heard?' said Diana in a slightly sneery voice. 'It's the British counterstrike. Last night Agent Z came through with the location of the French flagship *Titan*. Now the Royal Air Fleet are planning to launch a flotilla of warcraft to destroy her, before she's dressed in her Aetheric Shield. The French are constantly moving her about, so we've probably only got a few days.'

Not for the first time, Arabella felt distinctly out of the loop. She hadn't heard anything about this, and, from the look on her friend's face, neither had Cassie.

She was sure that Diana and Beatrice weren't officially privy to any more information than they were, but somehow they always seemed better informed – they were probably just better at keeping their ears to the ground.

'So you think the air fleet could be targeted by whoever's snatching all these airships?' Cassie asked Beatrice.

Diana put her finger to her lips. 'Let's change the subject. Here comes Emmeline.'

Arabella looked up and, sure enough, there was Aunt Emmeline – a tall, stern-looking young redhead – emerging from their hotel and crossing the street towards them. Emmeline was only a few years older than Arabella, but her ambition and ability had caught the eye of chief spymaster Sir George Jarrett, and she had swiftly risen to a senior rank in the British Imperial Secret Service. It was Emmeline who had urged Sir George to form the Sky Sisters. She'd argued that Britain should exploit its superiority in the new technology of heavier-than-air flight. A small team of female aviators, each specialising in a different skill, could get behind enemy lines, link up with anti-Bonapartists, uncover enemy secrets, take part in sabotage operations and generally disrupt the French military machine. Jarrett had been persuaded, and three years ago Emmeline recruited her first Sky Sister, Diana, quickly followed by Cassie and then Beatrice. Last year, she had completed the team by enlisting her niece, Arabella. The two had lived together since Arabella was twelve – the year her father had disappeared from her life – and Emmeline had watched her progress with interest. By the time Arabella was eighteen, Emmeline decided that her niece's spectacular flying skills could be put to good use in the service of their nation.

Emmeline was frowning when she reached them. She didn't need to say anything. One glance at the sky, which was rapidly filling up with storm clouds, told them all they needed to know: there would be no flying this afternoon. Arabella felt deflated. She'd been looking forward to practising some new manoeuvres in *Prince*.

'Sorry, Sisters,' said Emmeline. 'Tomorrow, maybe.'

'What shall we do instead?' wondered Cassie.

'Do you even need to ask?' cried Diana. 'This is Brighton! Why don't we start with a promenade on the pier? It's the place to see and be seen.'

'But spies aren't supposed to be seen,' pointed out Beatrice.

'Can't we have a day off?' moaned Diana.

'No,' said Emmeline. 'Besides, there's a storm brewing. I suggest we head back to the hotel for an early lunch.'

They were about to do so when their attention was caught by a commotion on the Chain Pier. A crowd had gathered on the western side, close to the beach. Many of them were shouting and gesturing at the sea.

Arabella looked towards where they were pointing and spotted a figure in a life-vest, afloat on the surf. The person looked unconscious or dead, battered by the waves and being pushed against the iron struts that formed the base of the pier.

CHAPTER SEVEN

THE
RESCUE

Without thinking, Arabella dropped the remains of her ice cream and flew down the concrete steps to the beach. She ran as fast as her high-heeled ankle boots would allow, across the pebbles towards the stranded figure. She could hear the heavy crunch of Cassie's footsteps behind her. As they ran, the first raindrops began wetting the pebbles and splattering the creamy surf. The drops quickly became a downpour, darkening the air and chilling her skin.

She ran down to where the sea crashed and foamed at her ankles. The wind howled, the sea hissed and salt spray stung her face, forcing her eyes almost closed, but she could see the figure more clearly now. It was a young man with a pale, bruised face, dark hair and beard. He was floating face up, eyes closed, mouth dangling open. The sea was pounding him repeatedly against the iron supports and their rough, barnacle-encrusted concrete base with a force that looked likely to break all his bones.

Arabella was about to wade in when she realised that her heavy clothing would soon drag her under. She quickly shrugged off her jacket, shawl, corset, skirt and petticoat, kicked off her boots and waded into the surf dressed only in her knee-length chemise. Glancing back, she saw Cassie following suit. Behind them, a small crowd of onlookers had gathered on the beach. From the esplanade above, Emmeline was waving at them, shaking her head. Arabella knew that what they were doing was strictly against the rules. The Sky Sisters were supposed to behave discreetly at all times, never drawing attention to themselves. But what could she do? Was she supposed to leave this poor man to drown?

She waved back at her boss, pretending not to understand, then plunged into the surf. The brine was icy against her skin and the stones were sharp against her feet, but Arabella had never been scared of physical discomfort – she knew deep-down-in-the-bones cold from winter flights above the Wadden Sea, on the northern limits of the French Empire. Her main fear was of losing her balance in the swell and being crushed against the rough concrete base of the pier. She let Cassie, who was bigger and stronger, move ahead, and was relieved to see her friend manage to clutch hold of the base and anchor her feet in the seabed. Cassie was then able to lean back and grab hold of Arabella before the waves could pick her up and thrust her against the concrete.

A giant wave blasted Arabella, filling her nose and mouth with foul-tasting salty water. She wiped her face with her forearm and blinked, then caught sight of the man, just yards away. They edged closer. Arabella reached for his arm, then lost her footing and her grip on the pier. She slipped and was suddenly submerged in cold greyness. Water surged into her surprised mouth, and she surfaced, spluttering, as Cassie grabbed her. On her next attempt, Arabella caught hold of the man's wrist and pulled him close. He was as white as a corpse, his face and body slack, his only movement caused by the buffeting of the sea. She braced herself for the disappointment – she'd done her best, but she'd been too late. He might have been dead for some time. On the chest of his life-vest was the Red Ensign of the British Merchant Air Fleet. A trading vessel must have gone down. She wondered how many of his comrades had also died.

Cassie and Arabella dragged the man back towards the shore. As they laid him down on the pebbles, they received a surprise: as his back hit the ground, the man immediately started coughing and retching. He proceeded to vomit up what seemed like gallons of water. Then he lay back down, breathing rapidly and staring anxiously about him. His eyes, so Arabella thought, seemed to glitter with some dark and terrifying awareness.

In her excitement, Cassie seized the man's hand. 'Good sir! You're alive! Heaven be praised!'

The man gaped into her broad, smiling face and seemed to believe he was seeing a monster. He cowered from her and bent his body into the shape of a newborn baby, turning to one side and covering his face with his forearms.

'No!' he screamed. 'Leave us! I'm dreaming! You cannot be! You monster! You fiend! Leave us!'

Cassie and Arabella stared at each other, as the rain hammered on the beach around them and the sea crashed in their ears.

CHAPTER EIGHT

THE SURVIVOR'S STORY

Two hours later, Arabella was starting to feel her fingers and toes again. She'd had a bath and dressed in dry clothes, and was about to head downstairs for luncheon when a hotel clerk brought an urgent message asking her to come to Emmeline's room. Arabella knew she was in trouble – Emmeline had disappeared from the scene without saying a word to her. She hoped she would understand that Arabella had acted from a deep instinct. Surely when a person's life is at stake, rules could and should be broken.

When she entered Emmeline's room, Arabella was surprised to see that her boss had been joined by two men, one of whom was the man they'd rescued. He was seated in a hunched posture on the chaise longue, his hands pressed tightly to his knees. He was dressed in a cheap, ill-fitting dark suit that must have only just been purchased for him. His complexion remained deathly pale, and his eyes were fixed on the wall directly in front of him, as if mesmerised by something only he could see. But at least he seemed calm.

The other man, like Emmeline, was standing. He was tall and entirely bald, with ice-blue eyes and a vivid white scar running from his cheekbone to the corner of his mouth. He was dressed entirely in black, and his hands were sheathed in black gloves. Arabella had rarely seen Sir George Jarrett in the flesh, but she recognised him instantly. He had visited her father once or twice at their house in Mayfair when she was a little girl, and his stern appearance had frightened her enough on those occasions to induce nightmares. Seeing him again now didn't scare her in the same way, but it made her anxious. She wondered what he was doing here. As Britain's spymaster-in-chief and a major target of Bonapartist assassins, Sir George had to live a very secretive life. Something extremely serious must have happened for him to appear in person like this.

Emmeline's greeting was stiff and formal. Arabella noticed the twitchiness of her hands as she gestured for her to take a seat.

Sir George bowed towards Arabella and offered her a thin, lopsided smile (the scarred side of his face seemed to be immobile). 'Good afternoon, my lady.

I remember meeting you when you were much younger. Your father was a good friend and a great man, and, from what I have been told of your exploits, you seem to be continuing the family tradition.'

Arabella tried to smile graciously. She never knew what to say or think when people spoke of her father. Her memories of him were so personal, it was sometimes hard to think of him as a public figure – a 'great man'. And when people compared her to him, it only made her feel awkward. She'd joined the flying corps of the secret service to feel closer to her father, and, when she was alone up there in the clouds, she often did. The trouble came down here on the ground – people expected her to be the new Lord Alfred West, and she could never be that; she could only be herself.

'You broke the rules this morning, Arabella,' said Emmeline. 'I understand why you acted as you did. All the same, the rules are there for a reason. We wouldn't be able to function without them. I had a struggle fending off the men from the press. Several of them were in the hotel lobby just now, demanding to know who you and Cassie were. They wanted your stories. I told them you were American tourists, currently on the Iron Horse Express bound for Vauxhall Aerodrome, after which you would be boarding the next flight to New York. I can only hope they believed me.'

Arabella looked penitently at her hands, folded in her lap. Inside, she felt anything but sorry. The man they had rescued was alive and breathing not ten feet from where Emmeline now stood. How could she possibly believe that his survival was not worth a few inconvenient questions from the local newshounds?

'As it happens, I didn't call you in to chastise you,' continued Emmeline. 'It turns out –'

Before she could say any more, there came a knock on the door, and in trooped Cassie, Diana and Beatrice.

'Ah, there you all are!' said Emmeline. 'Just in time.'

Arabella was amused by Cassie's look of complete shock when she saw the men in the room. Diana, however, seemed to take it all in her stride.

Sir George greeted them with a short bow. 'Ladies, it's a pleasure to meet you all at last,' he said. 'Emmeline has kept me abreast of your accomplishments, and may I say that Britain has much to be proud of.'

Cassie could only stare open-mouthed, while Beatrice nodded awkwardly and Diana made a graceful curtsey.

'I was about to say,' said Emmeline, turning towards the man on the chaise longue, 'that this gentleman, helped ashore by Cassie and Arabella this morning, has quite a tale to tell. If the press had shown the same interest in him as they showed towards his rescuers, they'd have had a *real* story on their hands.'

'Perhaps we should be grateful that they didn't,' said Sir George. 'We wouldn't want to start a general panic.' He crossed the room to where the other man was seated, then dropped to a crouch in front of him, blocking the patch of wall the fellow seemed so fascinated by. 'Mr Danforth!' he said in a loud voice. 'Would you mind repeating for those present the story you told us just now?'

The man jerked out of his trancelike state and focused on Sir George's face. The fear he had shown earlier on the beach returned to his features. But he wasn't reacting to the spymaster – it wasn't the scar or the Arctic-blue eyes that caused his mouth to twist or turned his eyes into big, dark, gleaming saucers. The fear seemed to come from within, from a memory that Sir George was asking him to recall.

'Mr Danforth!' said Sir George. 'You're a merchant airman, am I right? You were a crewman aboard the trading vessel HMAS *Borealis* that set out this morning from Folkestone, bound for West Africa.'

Danforth blinked and swallowed. His breathing slowed. Sir George's voice seemed to calm him. 'We was set fair,' he said in a voice that shook and creaked like an airship's suspension cable in a high wind. 'Makin' good time, we was. Launched at just after five o'clock this mornin' from Folkestone. Headin' west along the channel at forty knots, with a healthy tailwind. I was navigatin'. We was at fifty, fifteen, fifty-three north, zero, five, thirty-six west. Flyin' at three thousand feet. Scarcely a cloud in sight, clear from horizon to horizon... 'cept for one, that is, about a hundred or so feet above us. Strange-lookin' thing. Big and round, like a giant puffball. An' not movin' nor changin' shape, as clouds normally does. The wind were blowin', but that cloud, it stayed still as stone. An' then, out o' nowhere, it came…'

The man's mouth froze. His eyes became wide again, and searingly bright.

'What, Mr Danforth?' urged Sir George. 'What did you see?'

Danforth swallowed and tried again. 'Somethin' demonic came out o' that cloud, sir! I don't rightly know what it could have been. It looked like some sort of… bird, but that description don't do it justice. It were big – big as one o' them prehistoric beasts such as the Reverend Buckland's been diggin' up lately. Them dino-things.'

'Dinosaurs,' prompted Emmeline.

'That's right,' said Danforth. 'Like one of them, or maybe even bigger. And its wings…' What little colour there was in Danforth's cheeks drained away, and Arabella seriously thought he might faint. 'Its wings were wider and broader than our entire vessel, and when they stretched to their full extent, they cast a shadow deep as night over all of us. As this thing come screamin' down from out the cloud, I can't describe the terror that overtook us. It had this fearsome sharp beak that opened, showin' a tongue that seemed to drip with fire. It had talons bigger than elephant tusks, which it plunged into the fabric of our vessel. I felt a jolt like an earthquake, and our ship collapsed like a burst balloon. *But we didn't fall.*

'The thing had us, see? Secure as a newborn lamb in the jaws of a lion, and now we was risin'. Risin' toward the cloud! Some of my fellow crew screamed and leapt overboard, preferrin' to fall to their deaths from twenty thousand feet than be carried up into that cloud to be fed on at leisure by the monster. Others got down on their knees an' prayed. One man managed to inflate one of the lifecraft. There were scarce any time as we were closin' in on the cloud. Desperate men tried to scramble aboard the lifecraft, though there was places for six at most. Many lost their footin' or were pushed aside by other men and sent tumblin' to their deaths.' Danforth looked down at the floor and shook. 'I fear I may have been one of them doin' the pushin'. At least five or six I saw fall.

'In the end there was only two of us in the craft, and the other man untethered the rope. Matthew, his name was. Matthew Grimthorpe. Pleasant fellow. Big and handsome. He give me this grin as if to say, *we're goin' to make it, Ollie*. And then come this big *swoosh*, and the wing, the dark blade of this giant creature's wing, come slicin' through the air and... and took his head clean off his shoulders.

'I drifted for a league or more in my tiny airship, too stunned to move or think. At some point I believe I started cryin'. I forgot who I was, or where. Maybe an hour passed before I come to me senses. I saw the crests of the waves just a yard or so beneath me. I tried ventin' air from the ballonets to gain some height, but the creature had damaged the mechanism, and I knew I were going down. I put on me life-vest and waited for the waters to claim me. Then I swam until I had no strength left. I suppose the tide must have carried me ashore.'

'Thank you, Mr Danforth,' said Sir George gently.

CHAPTER NINE

THE
MISSION

Oliver Danforth looked utterly drained by the retelling of his tale. His head lolled and his eyes found another patch of empty wall to fix themselves on. Emmeline summoned a hotel clerk to escort him to the lobby. She assured him an ambulance would be along shortly to take him to the Sussex County Hospital for a full check-up.

Before Danforth left, Sir George took him firmly by the wrist and locked him in his glacial stare. 'Mr Danforth,' he said, 'if you care for your career prospects in the Merchant Air Fleet, I urge you not to repeat your story to anyone else, not even your own family.'

Danforth looked at him blankly for a second, then nodded.

When Danforth was gone, Sir George returned to his former spot by the window and stared out at the rain. Emmeline turned to the other Sisters. 'Well, you've heard what the man had to say. Does anyone have any comments?'

There was silence from the floor. Arabella didn't know what to make of Danforth's story, and there was no way she was going to risk blurting something out and making a fool of herself. Finally, Diana said: 'Clearly the man's a fantasist of the first order. A creature such as he described simply cannot exist.'

'I'm inclined to agree with your second point, but not necessarily your first,' said Emmeline. 'We've received reports from Folkestone that they lost aetherwave contact with the *Borealis* at 07:15 this morning, which would have been around the time the airship reached the coordinates Mr Danforth gave us just now. Air–Sea Rescue craft have been combing the seas south of here since 08:00, and have found no sign of the vessel. If this had been an accident, there would have been some wreckage to be seen on the surface, but nothing has been found. It seems that some sort of attack did take place. If we're agreed that nothing natural could match Danforth's description of this aerial predator, then we are forced to accept that it must have been a mechanical contrivance of some kind, a work of technology, a...'

'A new kind of weapon!' Sir George broke in, turning to face the room. He began pacing back and forth across the carpet and gesturing with his arms as he elaborated on this theory. 'We're well aware of how the human imagination can sometimes turn one thing into something else. The good folk who ply our trade routes by sea and air are especially prone to it. Mariners of old mistook sea cows for mermaids. More recently, our aircrewmen have observed lights in the sky and believed them to be visitors from another planet. In my view, something similar has happened in this case. A large air carriage, perhaps one decorated in fanciful paintwork, attacked the *Borealis* this morning. It must have been equipped with a grappling hook of some kind, which it used to burst the gas envelope before carrying the stricken vessel to a secret location…'

'For what purpose?' asked Cassie.

Sir George's eyebrows flickered in surprise. 'Why, I'd have thought that was obvious. The *Borealis* was carrying goods of some value. And we know there are pirates about. France's long campaign to subdue Norway has created large numbers of desperate refugees, some of whom have begun attacking our shipping and our coasts in the manner of their Viking ancestors.'

'Or there's another possibility,' said Emmeline. 'This could be a new piece of French technology designed to spread terror in our skies, softening us up ahead of their invasion.'

'That is certainly a possibility,' Sir George conceded. 'But this is all speculation. The honest truth is that we really don't know what attacked the *Borealis* – only that it fits an emerging pattern. This is the fourth airship to disappear this month, and the second in as many days. And we simply can't afford to let this continue…'

He stopped pacing and turned to face his audience, scrutinising each of the Sisters in turn. The ice-burn of his stare forced Arabella to look down at her feet. She sensed he was about to divulge some important and highly secret information.

'Some of you may already know about Operation Zeus, our planned counterstrike against the French invasion fleet.' Sir George's voice was little more than a whisper. 'In two days' time, at dawn on the 18th of July, HMAS *Nelson*, the flagship of the Royal Air Fleet, will take off from Weymouth in Dorset at the head of a squadron of warcraft, headed for the port of Granville in north-western France, where the French flagship, *Titan*, is presently located. Their mission is to destroy it. Nothing, and I mean *nothing*, must be allowed to go wrong with this operation. The French will be moving *Titan* again very soon, so we can't delay it. This – this aerial pirate ship, or whatever it is – must be dealt with before Operation Zeus takes place.'

Sir George consulted his pocket watch. 'I must go back to London now for a briefing with the prime minister. I will leave it to Emmeline to discuss tactics.' He began heading for the door, then turned as if

remembering something. 'You have two days, ladies –
two days to rid our skies of this menace. Your country
is depending on you as never before!'

CHAPTER TEN

THE
SEARCH

hree hours later, at just after 16:00, Arabella found herself in her favourite place in all the world – strapped into the cockpit seat of *Comanche Prince*. She was also in her favourite clothes – her beautiful leather aviator's jacket, baggy woollen trousers, leather boots, leather flying cap and goggles. *Prince*, now fully repaired after the Fontainebleau mission, had been recoated in glossy red paint. His wings shone prettily in the sun, now re-emerging from behind its mantle of raincloud.

Arabella taxied towards the runway of Shoreham Air Base. Behind her followed the other Sky Sisters in their own aerial steam carriages: Beatrice in her blue Double-Wing, *Rani of the Madurai*; Cassie in her green

Steam Glider, *Sultan of Mandara*; and Diana in her yellow Motorbird, *Amazon Queen*.

Emmeline, a formidable aviatrix herself, was not flying with them today. She had to be on the ground, liaising with London and updating Sir George with any news. As this was to be a purely aerial mission, Arabella, the next most experienced pilot, was placed in charge of the first stage – locating the target. Thereafter, she would relinquish authority to Diana. The thought of leading the Sisters on a mission filled Arabella with pride. She was the youngest and most recent recruit, so this was a major honour.

After receiving clearance for take-off, Arabella commenced her acceleration along the runway. There was a slight headwind, reducing the speed required for take-off. But this was balanced by the additional weight of eight .303-inch Jennings steam cannon attached to *Prince*'s wings. This mission was not just about reconnaissance – with less than two days to go before the launch of Operation Zeus, there was no time for that luxury. Their goal was to seek out the mysterious aerial predator and destroy it.

Adding further to *Prince*'s payload was a passenger – Miles, the Logical Englishman, whom Arabella had stowed in the compartment behind her cockpit. When Emmeline had questioned her niece on her reasons for taking him on an aerial mission, she had found it hard to answer. She could only say that her brief experience with him in Fontainebleau had taught her to trust him.

Negative and perpetually gloomy he might be, but his instincts had proved correct. Even when stowed away and out of sight, he had become, for her, a kind of talisman.

Arabella achieved lift-off at 65 mph, well clear of the end of the runway. With a touch more thrust, she increased her wings' angle of attack and began her steady climb towards the clouds. She levelled off at 1,500 feet and began to circle the aerodrome as she waited for the other Sisters to join her. Shoreham lay on the coast a little to the west of Brighton. Part of her orbit took her out over the sea, which glittered like a hard grey jewel beneath the silver-bright glare of the sun.

She took her readings (North 50° 50' 10.6786", West 0° 17' 41.0733"; east wind, gusting at 24 knots) and rechecked the coordinates Oliver Danforth had given them for the last known whereabouts of the *Borealis*. Using these, she calculated her heading at 156° 30' 31", roughly south-south-west, for a distance of 43 miles. If they averaged 120 mph, they'd be there in around 20 minutes.

Once the other Sisters were all airborne, she sent them the information on the aethercell and gave the order to form into a loose 'ladder', with Arabella in front and the others lining up to her right, each slightly behind the air carriage to their left. When she was satisfied with the formation, Arabella pointed *Prince*'s nose towards the sea's horizon, and the four air carriages began climbing to their normal cruising altitude of 2,000 feet.

As they flew out across the sea, Arabella allowed herself to contemplate the coming mission. What kind of danger were they heading into? What was this giant bird-machine that was powerful enough to carry off an entire cargo vessel in its talons? And what chance did she and her little troupe have against such a monster, if it existed? The wind-tossed clouds swirled about her like the fumes of an evil witch's brew, frequently shrouding Beatrice's blue *Rani* from her sight.

Arabella suddenly felt vulnerable – a girl in a tiny metal box, alone in a giant sky. Occasionally these fears struck her, and she did what she always did at such moments: she lost herself in her routines. Altitude, heading, velocity, wind speed. She checked and rechecked her instruments, not out of need, but simply for reassurance.

When they reached the location of the *Borealis's* disappearance, Arabella ordered the Sisters to fan out and circle the areas immediately east, south and west, while she concentrated on the area to the north. She'd decided to give them each their own sector in order to maximise the range of the search, knowing they only had sufficient fuel for half an hour, after which they'd be forced to return to base.

Conditions in the search area were no different from those everywhere else this afternoon. All traces of the storm had gone, and the wind gusting from the east was mild. The sun shone intermittently through patches of grey-white cloud. It was a normal, everyday sort of sky, like hundreds Arabella had flown through. There was no sign of the monster bird, nor the strange, unmoving cloud of Danforth's story. Arabella dropped to a lower altitude and studied the dark, twinkling surface of the sea. Perhaps the aerial searchers, out earlier in the day, had missed some wreckage. But no, the sea seemed as empty as the sky.

The thirty minutes passed quickly. None of the other Sky Sisters reported seeing anything, so Arabella gave the order to regroup in formation for the journey home. She was disappointed. To come across the giant mechanical beast would have been terrifying at first, but she was sure that her instincts and training would have quickly come to the fore, and she'd have gone in with steam cannon blazing. Now, she'd probably never get the chance. They'd failed, and Sir George would surely move on to Plan B: attempting to bait the monster by sending out a decoy cargo ship. The Sky Sisters wouldn't be part of that mission, sadly.

Diana and Cassie soon came into view, and the three of them circled while waiting for Beatrice. When she failed to show, Arabella contacted her again. Over the crackle of aethercell static, she heard Beatrice's voice, sounding unusually excited: 'I've seen the cloud!' she cried, and quickly gave her coordinates: 'North 50° 14′ 43.6146″, East 0° 7′ 8.8788″.'

'Let's go,' Arabella aethercelled the other two as she executed a banked turn. Beatrice was about a mile away to the south-east. They wouldn't have time to do more than observe the cloud and note its location, before heading home to refuel.

Twenty seconds later, a gauzy curtain of cirrus parted and there, below her, was Beatrice's blue Double-Wing, circling in the shadow of a massive cliff of thick, creamy cloud. The cloud-wall bulged gently, and so evenly that it appeared almost artificial. It curved away at the sides and base and – far above them – at the top, to form a tall, elongated sphere. It was denser than any cloud Arabella had ever encountered, with a texture that reminded her of mashed potato. And – as Oliver Danforth had said – it didn't move. Clouds moved around it, and buffeted and dispersed against its sides, but the giant cloud remained motionless and unchanged. So Danforth had been right about the cloud. That meant he was probably right about the monster-bird, too!

Diana's voice came on the aethercell: 'Good find, *Rani*. We know where it is now, and it doesn't look as if it's going anywhere. Let's return to base, stock up on coal powder, and return.'

'Negative, *Amazon Queen*,' Beatrice came back. 'I'm going in.'

Arabella stared in astonishment as Beatrice's Double-Wing looped back and headed straight into the base of the cloud, disappearing from view.

CHAPTER ELEVEN

THE CLOUD

'Rani,' cried Diana. 'Come in, *Rani*. I demand you return this instant.'

There was no reply from Beatrice – only static.

For a few seconds, no one reacted. Then Arabella found her hands moving the control stick and pushing forward on the throttle.

She was heading towards the cloud.

It was the same impulse that had carried her down onto the beach that morning – a drive so deep within her, she was helpless to control it. Bea was in danger – she had to go and help.

'*Comanche Prince*,' Diana's voice shouted over the aethercell. 'I'm now in charge of this mission and I'm ordering you back.'

Arabella ignored the message. She aimed a few yards above the hole that Beatrice's Double-Wing had torn in the strange, mushy fabric of the cloud – a hole, she noticed, that was already closing up, as if the cloud was repairing itself.

She plunged into the creamy wall and entered a white, silent world. Aethercell, engine, propellor – all sound ceased. Had she gone deaf? At the same time, the view outside the canopy became pure, unblemished white, as if she had crash-landed in a mountain of cotton wool. She didn't seem to be moving, yet she knew she had to be. One couldn't decelerate from 120 mph to zero in less than a second and survive.

The milky whiteness outside pressed in on the glass. It seemed so dense – more like a solid or liquid than a gas. If she opened the canopy, the stuff would surely pour in and fill the cockpit as well. She assumed she was still flying, yet without sight of her surroundings, how could she be sure? Shakily, she raised her aethercell to her mouth. '*Rani, Sultan, Amazon Queen*, this is *Comanche Prince*. Can you read me? Come in, please.'

Nothing.

Not even static.

Her instruments gave normal readings, but, oddly, the needles didn't wobble or flicker as they usually did – they were perfectly still. Everything seemed as it should be, yet dead. She bashed the instrument panel with her fist. Nothing. Not the smallest vibration. She tried applying the throttle. It made no change that she could feel.

Her fear pleaded with her to turn, turn, turn – get out of this nothing-world. Her hand squeezed the control stick, her feet strained to push on the rudder pedals. She was on the verge of turning around when, out of nowhere, she heard a voice: 'Hold your course, my darling. Be brave.'

Father!

His voice steadied her. She began breathing again. This would end – it had to end. This cloud couldn't go on forever.

And it didn't.

As suddenly as she'd entered the nothing-world, she was out of it. Sound returned – the friendly burble of her engine, the hiss of her aethercell, the whirr of her propeller. And light! She blinked in the silvery glow – not normal daylight; closer to bright moonlight.

Then something huge and dark reared up before her, making her gasp. She swerved hard to her left. Sparks flashed, and a grinding vibration ran through Prince as his starboard wing received a glancing blow.

She wheeled to gain some distance from the object, and saw, ahead of her, the strange cloud again – only this time its wall was concave. So then the cloud was hollow, and she was now inside it!

Arabella continued her long, shallow turn, skimming the edge of the cloud-wall with her wingtip before wheeling back to face the interior of the sphere.

In full view, ahead of her, floated the object she had, just now, so nearly collided with.

For a moment, she was confused. Had she dropped a couple of thousand feet to sea level without realising it? Was this some monstrous ocean liner steaming towards her? But a glance beneath Fit told her otherwise: it wasn't floating on water, but on air.

The bottom half was a gleaming bowl of metal, perhaps a third of a mile across. The bowl supported what appeared to be a small, circular city in the sky. The city soared above her in tier upon tier of buildings. The buildings, wide and low-rise at the edges, grew ever taller and narrower the closer they got to the middle, roughly following the contours of a hemisphere. The strange light inside the cloud was bright enough to see by, yet lights gleamed from many of the buildings' windows. Winding through and around each building, like ribbons of fettuccine, were walkways on which she could see, even from this distance, tiny figures moving. The roofs of the buildings formed terraces where more people could be seen wandering about among the chimneys that belched dark smoke towards the upper reaches of the cloud sphere. Some of the roofs had gardens growing on them, with trees, shrubs and lawns, as well as creepers that dangled over the edges, curtaining the windows of the buildings beneath. Evenly spaced around the circumference of the city were five tall, narrow towers, each of which supported a huge spinning propeller. Arabella could only assume that these giant propellers were the devices that kept the city afloat.

As she flew, awestruck, towards this metropolis, dozens of little hatches slid open in its metal hull, and from each of these emerged the snout of a cannon. Their muzzles flashed angrily, and suddenly the air around her erupted with whistles and bangs. Jolted out of her stupor, Arabella pulled hard to her left, then swooped, rolled and turned, so she was flying back towards the cloud wall. As she did so, she caught sight of *Rani* directly above her. Shockingly, her wing was on fire and she was falling in a steep dive, trailing thick black smoke. Arabella raced towards the stricken air carriage, but could only stare, appalled, as it disappeared into the thick white fog that formed the base of the cloud sphere.

She was about to follow Beatrice down when something flashed in the corner of her eye. The subsequent bang was so loud she feared it might shatter the glass of her canopy. A millisecond before the explosion, Arabella had already begun looping upwards. As *Prince* arched towards vertical, she felt the vibration of a projectile passing within yards of her. She half-completed the loop, so *Prince* was flying upside down, then rolled to an upright position. Below her, the guns were now firing constantly, filling the air with cracks, thumps and sulphurous smoke. It would be impossible to weave through all that lethal fire to get to the bottom of the sphere. She whispered a tearful 'sorry' to Bea, and prayed her comrade had managed to eject before plummeting into the English Channel.

Arabella had no choice but to flee from the cloud as quickly as she could. Her engine was already making irregular pops, a sure sign that it was low on fuel. She flew towards the cloud wall, but before she could reach it, a great shadow fell across her cockpit. She looked up – and screamed.

CHAPTER TWELVE

THE BIRD

Descending upon her was the most terrifying thing she'd ever seen. It resembled a giant eagle, but made entirely of metal. She could see the riveted sections of its skull-like head thrust forward on its powerful neck, the iron glint of its wing feathers. Its eyes, which burned red, were like glowing beads, fixed on her as if she were already its meal. Its sharply curved beak, slightly open, revealed strings of glowing white saliva. The bird shrieked as it swooped, drowning out her own sobs of fear. It arched its back, lowering its jointed legs and spreading its fiercely pointed talons towards her.

In desperation, Arabella banked right, just as a talon the same size as *Prince* slashed the air only inches from her port wing. She went into a tight spin, then manoeuvred herself into an upward spiral, hoping the bird's downward momentum would carry it beyond her. It seemed to work. She was ascending on full throttle, g-forces pressing down on her like physical weights. Her head pounded and her hands felt slippery with sweat. But the cloud wall was just fifty yards away and closing. She was going to make it...

Then an ear-shattering squawk from below made her jump six inches in her seat. The metal raptor reared up before her. Its wings spread to their full, immense span, blocking her escape. Its beak gaped to reveal a black tongue boiling in pinkish-white fire. The fire bloomed out towards her, blackening the top of her canopy and scorching the air inside the cockpit. Arabella screamed again. She felt as though she was burning – her goggles seemed to be melting on her face. Shoving hard on the control stick, she dived blind, somehow managing to fly straight between the bird's legs. Then she pulled up in the steepest possible ascent. *Prince* was an arrow, shooting vertically upwards. Arabella's muscles were strained to the maximum; her head felt ready to explode; the world, through the warped lenses of her goggles, became a blurry darkness. But she kept in the manoeuvre, pulling back, back, until she was upside down, with the bird beneath her. Three-quarters of the way through the loop, Arabella's thumb found the firing button at the top of the control stick. At forty-five degrees off horizontal, as the bird came back into view, she began firing. Two of the shells blasted against the iron feathers of the eagle's chest, sending it flapping backwards. Without waiting to see what damage she'd inflicted, she flew on past it, banking slightly to avoid one of its outstretched wings. This time, nothing would prevent her escape. She was closing in on the cloud wall – closing… closing…

Clang!

The sound and vibration shook her like the clapper of a bell. Her head banged painfully against the canopy window. Blinking, determined to stay conscious, Arabella tried to keep flying. She steered, but *Prince* didn't respond. She pulled on the throttle, making her engine pop feverishly and her propeller twirl faster, but *Prince* didn't move an inch. A feeling of dread overcame her as she raised her eyes. Through the charred glass, she could see the tips of six metallic talons hooked onto her wings, three on each side.

The bird had caught her!

Above the talons swelled the eagle's great metallic chest and beak. Over all of this, like two enormous black death-shrouds, beat its colossal metal wings. Arabella glimpsed complex machinery at work on their undersides – drive belts and gears turning, crank shafts rotating and huge pistons pumping. She could hear the hiss of gas expulsions as the bird carried her higher and higher.

Realising she was beaten, she relinquished the controls and leaned back in her seat, pushing up her goggles and wiping her face with her sleeve. Her head hurt and her cheeks felt tender where the goggles had burned them. For a while she could do nothing but breathe. Action, even thought, seemed beyond her.

Gradually her mind came back to life, as the view through the window piqued her curiosity. They were approaching the sky citadel. As they drew closer, details became apparent. The buildings, she noticed, were not the smooth, gleaming, futuristic towers they had seemed from a distance. In fact, they were were a ramshackle assortment of odd materials, salvaged from many different places, and nailed or welded together to make walls, windows and roofs. She spotted walls incorporating bathtubs and parts of steam carriages and giant cogs from factory engines. She saw roofs with guns poking out of steel turrets and houses made from the curved wooden hulls of airship gondolas. Even the tallest buildings, in the city centre, were not actually very tall – they had merely been built on top of the ones beneath. The city was, in fact, a giant hill of oddly constructed houses, all built on top of each other. And the twisting network of roads that ran through and between them was little more than a tangle of bumpy, potholed tracks. Even the gardens, which had seemed so impressive from a distance, were, on closer inspection, weed-infested patches of dirty grass overgrown with wild-looking trees and bushes. The creepers dangled over the roof edges like curtains because no one had ever pruned them.

If the city appeared odd, its inhabitants were like none she'd ever encountered. A crowd of them had gathered on a rooftop terrace not far from the city centre, and it was towards here that the bird seemed to be heading. The men in this welcoming party wore their hair long and their beards straggly. Their clothes were ill-fitting and in a whole ragbag of styles, with no thought to what went with what. She saw one fellow in striped trousers with an army jacket and a top hat, and another in a frock coat with knee-breeches and a straw boater. And the women were no better: she spotted several in tatty-looking evening dresses, with stained aprons and frilly maids' caps, not to mention eye patches. Indeed, quite a number of both the men and women were carrying serious injuries. Arabella counted at least half a dozen patched eyes and a hook for a hand. The hook was being waved cheerfully in the air as she and the bird came in to land.

CHAPTER THIRTEEN

THE SKY MAGISTER

The bird set her down surprisingly gently in the middle of the terrace – a flat roof of pale, weather-beaten wooden boards, interrupted by several tall smokestacks. Arabella remained where she was, in the sanctuary of her cockpit, looking nervously at the curious ragtag crowd outside as they surged closer.

From above, there came a great creaking of gears and a hiss of steam. She glanced up to see the talons opening and the huge wings beating with a force powerful enough to blow the hats off several onlookers. Then the mighty eagle took off. It circled the terrace once before disappearing from view. Its task was complete – it had captured her and brought her to this strange place. Now she was entirely at the mercy of its even stranger populace. What would they do to her? Tear her to pieces as soon as she stepped out? Turn *Prince* into scrap material for another of their ridiculous buildings? The signs were not promising. Already the braver ones were stroking the wings and the fuselage with their grimy fingers, and grinning at their friends. In doing so, they displayed many a yellow and broken tooth. These people may have engineered a floating city, but clearly they had yet to master basic dentistry.

She grabbed the daguerreotype of her father from where she'd pinned it above the control panel and stuffed it in the pocket of her jacket – these savages might take *Prince* from her, but they would have to prise that image from her dead fingers.

The mob was pressing closer, and it seemed only a matter of time before one of them jumped up and ripped open the canopy, when suddenly everyone's attention was diverted by a commotion on the far side of the terrace. A path opened up in the crowd and into it strode a man – a hugely impressive man, was Arabella's first thought. He was tall, and made taller by the battered tricorn hat perched on his head. His beard was short and well trimmed, but his hair was long and formed into matted coils, decorated with colourful beads that dangled across his shoulders. Those shoulders were broad, and made broader by his armour that rose up in wings above each arm. The armour was made from overlapping leather plates fixed with metal rivets. Dirty chain mail cloaked one powerful forearm, while the other was covered only with colourful tattoos.

His appearance reminded Arabella of a character from one of the fantasy tales her father used to tell her when she was little – a swashbuckling pirate king, perhaps. Only this king was no fairytale fantasy. There was nothing gentle or sweet about him. She shivered under his cold gaze and brutal sneer. His posture, hands on hips and legs akimbo, spoke of a master surveying his latest slave.

The pirate king nodded at one of the men in the crowd, and the fellow immediately clambered onto *Prince*'s wing and pulled open the canopy. As the outside air rushed into the cockpit, Arabella was confronted by a powerful odour of coal smoke, sweat and decaying food, reminding her of a busy London street on a Saturday afternoon. It saddened her that the pristine sky – the last pure place on Earth – had been polluted by this unwholesome city in the clouds. But this was, in truth, the least of her worries. Right now, her most immediate concern was for her own safety. The man who'd opened the canopy stood above her, cackling with mirth, and for one very scary moment Arabella wondered if she might be bodily dragged from the cockpit and immediately executed.

But the minion jumped down off the wing, and the pirate king stepped forward. 'Welcome, pretty lady!' he said in a surprisingly soft voice. 'I am Sky Magister

Odin, lord and master of all you see around you. Who, pray tell, are you?'

Arabella was unnerved by his voice – its velvety politeness seemed strained, as if he was suppressing a deep inner rage that might flare up at any moment.

'Lady Arabella West,' she answered as firmly as she could manage, then added her standard cover story: 'I am one of the Sky Sisters, an all-female aerobatic troupe.'

Odin seemed to find this amusing. He rubbed his chin and smirked. 'Aerobatic troupe? You're a little far from the paying public up here. Who were you planning on entertaining?'

'We were on an exercise...' Arabella began, before deciding that sounded a little too military. 'I mean to say, we were practising... our routines. And one of my team found this – this cloud. I followed her in. Now, if you'll let me go, I think she's in need of rescuing.'

Odin laughed. It was a mean, bullying kind of laugh, and it triggered a smattering of echoing chuckles and sniggers in the crowd.

'You're not going anywhere, *Lady* Arabella West,' he said, placing a mocking emphasis on her title.

These words seeped into her like acid, eating away at her confidence. 'Then am I to understand that I am your prisoner, sir?' she asked weakly.

'That is most certainly a fair understanding of the situation,' Odin replied, grinning at the crowd and provoking more raucous laughter.

Arabella swallowed. She had no defence against this man. Her position was hopeless. So she did what she'd always done, since childhood, when powerless: she started demanding things. 'Well, in that case,' said Arabella, 'I demand to know where I am. What is this place? Even a prisoner has the right to know that much.'

This only produced more amusement, and Arabella started to wonder whether her only purpose among these people was to provide comic relief.

'A prisoner with rights?' chortled the Sky Magister. 'Whatever will those Earthbound folk think of next?'

Then he became serious, and the throng quietened.

'I was Earthbound once, before any of this existed.' He gestured to his kingdom with a sweep of his tattooed arm. 'I was an admiral in the Norse fleet, fighting Boney, keeping him from our fjords. But a trivial incident led to my dismissal, and all of a sudden I was out – a man of energy and vision, but no flag under which to fight. Naturally, I turned to piracy – made a decent living, plundering ships and raiding coasts from Tromsø to Stavanger, Eastbourne to Inverness. Then, one day, my crew and I were captured by an English captain, a savage and remarkable man by the name of Allenson. For eight days he tortured us, finding the most imaginative ways to inflict pain. Out of one hundred and twenty-three men, only two survived the ordeal – myself and my bosun, Commodus Bane. The captain so admired our resilience that he set us free...

Bane and I each learned something from our time
with Allenson. Bane learned that there are no limits to
human savagery – a lesson he carries with him to this
day. As for me, I learned that I would sooner die than
fall under the power of another man.'

As he told his story, Odin's eyes turned inwards.
His face became tight with deeply buried rage, and
for a while he seemed to forget who he was talking to.
Then his mind resurfaced, and he turned to Arabella:
'Welcome, lady, to Taranis. Here, I am beholden to
no man. The French, the British, the Norse – they
have no claim on me. I'm free to pursue my dreams
of wealth and power. I and my Taranites can wander
wheresoever we please. We can plunder the world's
skyfaring vessels for food and treasure, and exploit
their crews for labour. We've crisscrossed the planet
in our protective cloud – the Americas, the East Indies,
the South China Sea. And now we're back on my home
patch, and it's the turn of you Brits to feel the blade of
our sky city at your throats. You want to know where
you are, Lady Arabella? The name is Taranis. It can
mean *freedom*, or it can mean *fear*, depending on your
perspective.'

Arabella didn't know how to respond to this, so she
said nothing.

Odin came closer and ran his fingers admiringly
over *Prince*'s bright red paintwork. 'So, you're an
artiste of the air,' he murmured. 'I enjoyed watching
your performance just now. The way you evaded our

Dread Eagle was... impressive. You have talent. Tell me, how long have you been flying with your troupe?'

'For about a year,' replied Arabella.

'A year?' Odin nodded thoughtfully. He continued to stroke the air carriage as if it were a horse he was admiring. 'And do you do many shows around the country?'

'Three or four a month during the summer season.'

Odin looked at her.

'Liar!' he suddenly screamed. He leapt onto the wing and hauled Arabella out of the cockpit. He pulled her up by her collar, so she was inches from his face and could smell the burnt onions and coffee on his breath.

Then he threw her down. She tried to grab hold of the aetherwave antenna behind the cockpit, but missed and tumbled painfully to the wooden floor below. Pain blazed through her shoulder as she hit the ground. She closed her eyes and bit her lip, refusing to cry out.

Odin had jumped back to the ground and was now glaring at her while pointing at the Jennings steam cannon fixed below her wings. 'I suppose this is part of your act, hmm?' he bellowed. 'When you've finished thrilling the crowds with your flick rolls and your loop-the-loops, you dive-bomb them, right? Now tell me the truth, lady. You're working for the British Imperial Secret Service, aren't you? You and your fellow aviators were on a mission to seek me out – to destroy me. Am I right?'

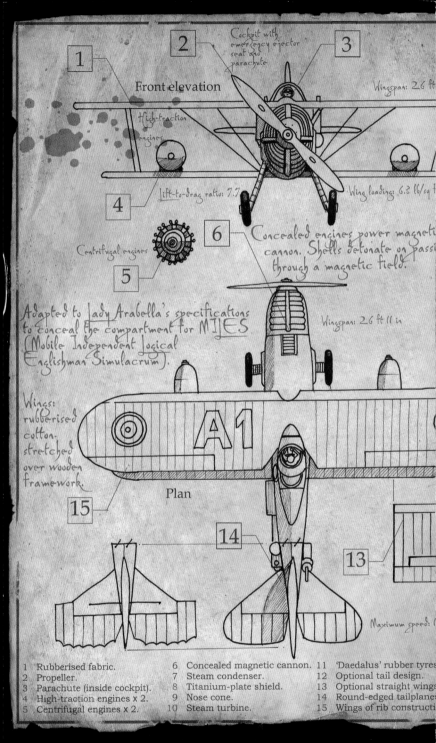

Front elevation

Cockpit with emergency ejector seat and parachute

Wingspan: 26 ft

1

2

3

High-traction engines

Lift-to-drag ratio: 7.7

Wing loading: 6.3 lb/sq f

4

Centrifugal engines

5

6

Concealed engines power magneti cannon. Shells detonate on passi through a magnetic field.

Wingspan: 26 ft 11 in

Adapted to Lady Arabella's specifications to conceal the compartment for MILES (Mobile Independent Logical Englishman Simulacrum).

Wings: rubberised cotton-stretched over wooden framework.

15

A1

Plan

14

13

Maximum speed:

1 Rubberised fabric.
2 Propeller.
3 Parachute (inside cockpit).
4 High-traction engines x 2.
5 Centrifugal engines x 2.

6 Concealed magnetic cannon.
7 Steam condenser.
8 Titanium-plate shield.
9 Nose cone.
10 Steam turbine.

11 'Daedalus' rubber tyres
12 Optional tail design.
13 Optional straight wings
14 Round-edged tailplanes
15 Wings of rib constructi

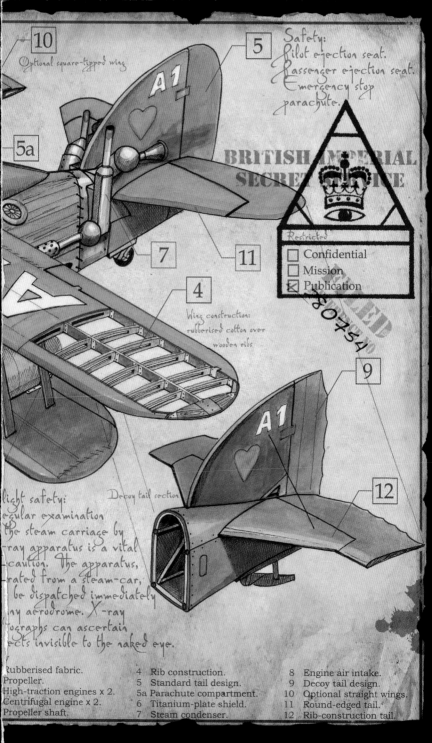

10 — Optional square-tipped wing

5

Safety:
Pilot ejection seat.
Passenger ejection seat.
Emergency stop parachute.

5a

7

11

4

Wing construction: rubberised cotton over wooden ribs

BRITISH IMPERIAL SECRET SERVICE

Restricted

- [ ] Confidential
- [ ] Mission
- [x] Publication

9

12

Flight safety:
...egular examination
...the steam carriage by
...-ray apparatus is a vital
...caution. The apparatus,
...rated from a steam-car,
...be dispatched immediately
...ny aerodrome. X-ray
...ographs can ascertain
...cts invisible to the naked eye.

Decoy tail section

...Rubberised fabric.	4 Rib construction.	8 Engine air intake.
...Propeller.	5 Standard tail design.	9 Decoy tail design.
...High-traction engines x 2.	5a Parachute compartment.	10 Optional straight wings.
...Centrifugal engine x 2.	6 Titanium-plate shield.	11 Round-edged tail.
...Propeller shaft.	7 Steam condenser.	12 Rib-construction tail.

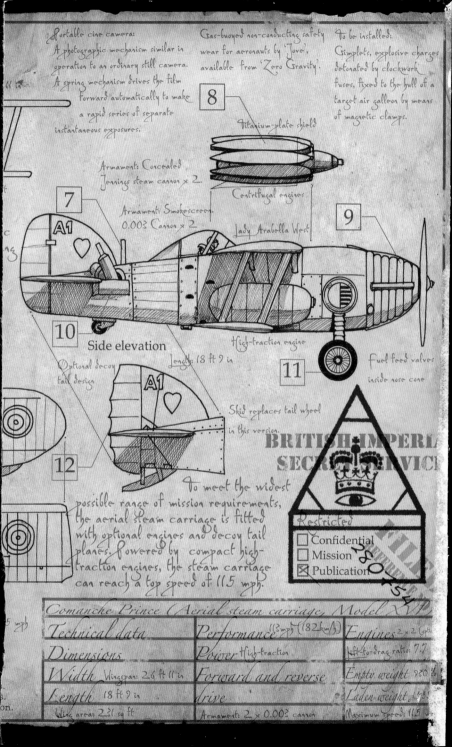

Portable cine camera:
A photographic mechanism similar in
operation to an ordinary still camera.
A spring mechanism drives the film
   forward automatically to make
      a rapid series of separate
instantaneous exposures.

Gas-buoyed non-conducting safety
wear for aeronauts by 'Jove',
available from 'Zero Gravity'.

To be installed:
Gimplets, explosive charges
detonated by clockwork
fuses, fixed to the hull of a
target air galleon by means
of magnetic clamps.

8

Titanium-plate shield

Armament: Concealed
Jennings steam cannon x 2.

Centrifugal engines

7

Armament: Smokescreen.
0.003 Cannon x 2

Lady Arabella West

9

A1

High-traction engine

10

Side elevation

Length: 18 ft 9 in

11

Fuel feed valves
inside nose cone

Optional decoy
tail design

A1

Skid replaces tail wheel
in this version.

12

To meet the widest
possible range of mission requirements,
the aerial steam carriage is fitted
with optional engines and decoy tail
planes. Powered by compact high-
traction engines, the steam carriage
can reach a top speed of 115 mph.

BRITISH IMPERIAL
SECRET SERVICE

Restricted
☐ Confidential
☐ Mission
☒ Publication

280 754

Comanche Prince (Aerial steam carriage, Model XVI)		
Technical data	Performance 113mph (182 km/h)	Engines 2 x 2 (x4)
Dimensions	Power High-traction	lift-to-drag ratio: 7.7
Width Wingspan: 26 ft 11 in	Forward and reverse	Empty weight 980 lb
Length 18 ft 9 in	drive	Laden weight 1,450
Wing area: 231 sq ft	Armament: 2 x 0.003 cannon	Maximum speed: 115

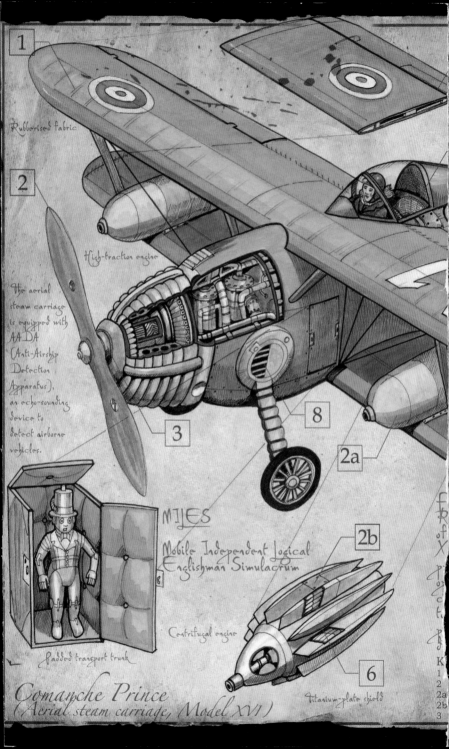

1

Rubberised fabric

2

High-traction engine

The aerial
steam carriage
is equipped with
AADA
(Anti-Airship
Detection
Apparatus),
an echo-sounding
device to
detect airborne
vehicles.

3

8

2a

MILES

Mobile Independent Logical
Englishman Simulacrum

Padded transport trunk

2b

Centrifugal engine

6

Titanium-plate shield

*Comanche Prince
(Aerial steam carriage, Model XVI)*

CHAPTER FOURTEEN

THE NEW ARRIVAL

Sky Magister Odin crouched beside the prostrate Arabella. He drew a knife from his belt and held the point close to her throat. In a disconcertingly calm voice, he whispered: 'I've got little use for you, Lady Arabella. Your air carriage may have some parts we can exploit. But you? You're a frail-looking thing and, after our capture of the *Borealis* this morning, we've got our full complement of slave labour. The only reason you're still breathing is because I think you've got some information in that pretty head of yours – information that I could use. So tell me, are you or are you not a spy?'

With a gleaming blade at her throat it was hard for Arabella to think clearly. 'I – I'm an aviator, a stunt pilot,' she stammered. 'The guns are… part of our act. We shoot at dummy targets. We…' She felt the knife point cutting her skin, and stopped talking.

'Shut up!' Odin shouted. 'Just shut up with your stupid lies. I know that a man escaped the *Borealis*. He must have got to shore and alerted your government. Or else why would four armed air carriages pitch up a few hours later at this particular location? So please don't waste any more of my time. Just admit that you're a spy and tell me what I need to know.'

He leaned in very close and murmured: 'My sources inform me that in thirty-six hours' time, you Brits are launching a strike against Boney's invasion fleet. Among the forces being dispatched will be HMAS *Nelson*, flagship of the Royal Air Fleet – a vessel I plan to capture.'

Arabella tried to suppress her shock at these words. 'I don't know what you're talking about,' she murmured.

The point dug deeper into her neck. She could feel a trickle of blood on her skin. *Don't lose hope,* she told herself. Diana and Cassie must surely be back at Shoreham by now. They'd soon be returning with an armoured fleet…

Odin's face loomed large above her. 'Don't bother dreaming of rescue, lady,' he said, as if he'd just climbed inside her mind. 'Do you think we'd stay in the same location long enough to be found? There are rudders and propellers at the base of this city constantly shifting us from place to place. How else could we have stayed undiscovered for this long? Now... why don't you be a sensible girl and tell me the route of the *Nelson*? Where's it leaving from? Where's it heading?'

'I don't know what you're —'

'Because if you don't tell me, I'll have to send you to Commodus Bane, and trust me, you do not want to meet that man.'

From somewhere close by, a low chant started up in the crowd:

Commodus Bane, the man is insane!
Commodus Bane, he knows about pain!

'We've captured some brave men and women in our time on Taranis,' breathed Odin. 'But Dr Bane broke them all in the end. So don't try to be brave, Lady Arabella...'

Just then there came the sound of running footsteps. 'Sky Magister! Sky Magister!' came a breathless voice.

Odin looked up. 'What is it?'

'An air carriage is approaching, sir.'

Hearing this, Arabella's heart quickened. They'd found her!

'What sort of air carriage?' demanded Odin.

'You can see it from here, sir,' said the messenger. He was wearing a shabby military coat and a peaked cap that barely contained his thatch of straw-coloured hair. Odin grabbed a telescope from the man and put it to his eye.

As Arabella tried to rise, her arm was immediately grabbed by a burly-looking fellow, the same one who'd originally jumped onto *Prince*'s wing. His grip tightened painfully as she tried to pull away. 'Come wi' me,' he ordered, and he dragged her to the precipice at the edge of the rooftop, where Odin and the rest of the crowd had gathered to get a better view of the approaching craft.

Standing on tiptoes to see past those in front, she spotted, far below, a single-engine air carriage flying towards the widest part of Taranis, where the bowl-shaped metal hull met the base of the city. It wasn't quite the armoured fleet she'd been hoping for. In fact, it was one of the least impressive aerial machines she could ever remember seeing. Battered and torn and coughing like an early-model steam-bike, it appeared to be something put together with patches of cloth and piano wire by a Sunday afternoon hobbyist. She was frankly amazed that such a contraption had got off the ground, let alone made it all the way up here.

'It's flying the colours of a merchant trader,' muttered Odin, still peering through his telescope.

'Shall we open fire, sir?' asked the messenger.

'No,' said Odin. 'Let it land. Then escort the pilot directly to me. If he's got something to sell, I want to see it first.'

They all watched as the tiny craft came down, bumping and skidding along the flat circular road that marked the outer edge of the city.

While everyone waited for the visitor to be brought before Odin, Arabella again tried to tug her arm free, which only provoked her captor to grip her even more tightly. 'You're going nowhere, girl,' he hissed cheerfully through his revolting teeth.

Ten minutes later, a door opened on the far side of the terrace and out stepped a tall young lad, flanked by two grey-uniformed Taranite guards. At the sight of him, Arabella's stomach did a double looping inverted barrel roll, the like of which even she would never have attempted as a pilot. The boy was wearing a grubby, double-breasted military jacket, coloured the blue of the US Army and complete with gold epaulettes. The top three buttons were open and around his neck he had knotted an oil-stained red scarf. His flying goggles were pushed up onto his forehead, revealing the full splendour of his 'intense, dark eyes'.

Ben Forrester!

CHAPTER FIFTEEN

THE AETHERIC SHIELD GENERATOR

The American mercenary was the last person Arabella had ever expected or, indeed, desired to see. The British government might have declared him the single most wanted individual on the planet since his theft from her, six weeks ago, of the formula for the Aetheric Shield, but as far as Arabella was concerned, he was quite the reverse. It was pure physical weakness on her part that her stomach had done that odd aerobatic manoeuvre on seeing him, and it did not detract one iota from her utter contempt for the young war profiteer.

Disconcertingly, it appeared from the way he was smiling at her that the feeling was not exactly mutual. He raised his hand in greeting.

'Your ladyship! How're you doing?'

Arabella coloured and looked down. The safest thing would be to pretend complete ignorance of their acquaintance.

Odin glanced suspiciously at the pair of them.

'You can put that down right there,' said Ben to a third guard, staggering along behind him under the weight of a metal box. With a sigh, the guard dropped it on the wooden decking. 'Careful, mister!' chided Ben. 'There's a lot of expensive kit in there.'

'Do you two know each other?' demanded a frowning Odin.

Ben smiled at Arabella in the manner of an old friend. 'Oh yeah! We worked together on a little project in France recently. We made a fine team, wouldn't you agree, ma'am?'

'Is she a spy?' Odin challenged him.

Ben hesitated a moment, and Arabella's heart skipped several beats. He frowned, as if baffled by the question. 'I don't believe so,' he replied eventually. Then he grinned and treated her to a wink. 'But you never can tell these days, can you?'

Odin grunted in a dissatisfied sort of way. His eye fell on the metal box. 'How did you find us?'

Ben laughed, and didn't seem too concerned when no one joined in, or when the mood of the crowd grew, if anything, a few degrees chillier. Odin himself looked about ready to boil over with anger at the boy's impudence.

'You'll never guess,' said Ben. 'I was travelling from Fécamp to Worthing – on business, you understand – when I happened upon this big, smooth cloud, shaped like an oversize soccer ball. And I thought to myself, Ben, I thought… That's my name, by the way – Ben Forrester. Pleased to meet y'all.' He grinned and took a small bow. 'So I thought to myself, this is not a cloud fashioned by nature. And if nature did not fashion it, then it must be the work of human beings. Now, being a man of finely honed commercial instincts, I reasoned to myself that where there are human beings, there is usually money to be made, and this was not an opportunity any right-minded businessman ought to pass up –'

'Enough of this!' Odin finally bellowed.

A grey-bearded guard clouted Ben hard across the cheek, making the boy stagger a little and clutch his face. 'You are in the presence of Odin,' the guard barked at him, 'Sky Magister of Taranis. You will show respect when you speak to him. You will not laugh, and your answers will be brief and to the point.'

Odin came closer to Ben, scrutinising him. 'State the nature of your business, American. Say it in *one* sentence, or I'll make you walk the plank. It's a short plank on this ship, but a long drop beneath it.'

Ben frowned at this challenge. He started to speak, then thought better of it. He held up a forefinger and mouthed *One sentence?!* as if to check that the Sky Magister had really meant it. Then he scratched his head and lapsed into thought. There was a bravado about his performance that Arabella couldn't help admiring. The young man might have the morals of a jackal, but she couldn't deny that he also had courage.

'I want to sell you indestructibility,' said Ben, finally.

Odin raised an eyebrow. 'Indestructibility?'

'Indeed,' nodded Ben. 'In this box, sir, is an Aetheric Shield Generator.'

These words shocked Arabella to the core and instantly obliterated any burgeoning sympathy she might have felt for Ben Forrester. He was selling the Aetheric Shield to a bunch of common pirates!

'If you'll allow me to demonstrate,' said Ben, squatting down to open the box. The crowd shuffled closer, eager to see what this 'indestructibility' machine looked like.

Ben carefully removed a device from the interior of the box. It consisted of a fine-looking cube of polished rosewood, supported on four delicately crafted bronze feet. A small bronze tube, like a miniature cannon, projected from one of its sides. Positioned on top of the cube were five iron towers, each about eight inches high, arranged in a circle around a small, bronze-rimmed hole in the cube's surface. A coil of copper wire was tightly wound around each of the towers.

Ben pointed to the towers. 'These, my friends, are electromagnets, arranged in such a way that, at a certain frequency, they will open up a portal into the Aethersphere.'

There were murmurs in the crowd at the mention of that mysterious realm, the Aethersphere. Despite herself, Arabella felt a prickling of interest. Aether, as every schoolchild knew, was the invisible medium through which everything travelled, including light, sound, physical objects, perhaps even thought. But no one knew what aether actually was. Just five years ago, British scientist John Payne had been experimenting with electromagnets when he accidentally discovered the Aethersphere, a dimension made entirely of aether. Researchers were still no closer to understanding the nature of aether, though it soon became clear that there was a constant flow of this substance between the Aethersphere and our world. The Aethersphere fascinated scientists, engineers and philosophers, but they could find no practical use for it – until Bonaparte's technologists had created the Aetheric Shield Generator…

Ben explained: 'The Aetheric Shield Generator works by passing gold particles through the Aethersphere. This creates bubbles of aetheric energy that will project from here…' He pointed to the small bronze cannon protruding from the side of the cube. 'The bubbles will surround the object you wish to protect and make it impervious to any weapon.'

Odin stepped closer to the device, surveying it with a sceptical eye. 'Are you seriously expecting me to believe that a little thing like that could protect my city?'

Ben shook his head. 'I'm a salesman, Mister Sky Magister sir, and I know that some of my kind will say pretty near anything to make a sale, but I for one will not make a claim that isn't the God's honest truth, and I can tell you now, sir, that it would take a machine at least a hundred times bigger than this one, and more gold than there is in all of California, to protect your entire city. But if you're talking about protecting something a little smaller, like a human being for instance – if you wanted, say, a personal shield to protect your good self, sir – then that is well within the capabilities of my machine.'

Odin nodded thoughtfully. 'Prove it.'

'Certainly.' Ben knelt down next to his metal box. Inside its lid was a panel of dials and indicator displays. He used a wire to connect this to the Aetheric Shield Generator, then flipped a switch on the panel. The device began to hum, and the needles on the displays flickered to life. He adjusted some dials, and the humming increased in volume and began buzzing and squeaking like an aetherwave receiver being tuned. The sound finally stabilised as a hissing crackle, and, before the startled eyes of the observers, something very strange appeared in the air between the five electromagnetic towers.

CHAPTER SIXTEEN

THE DEMONSTRATION

The most one could say about it was that it was a shape of some kind – perhaps a ball, perhaps a cube, or perhaps something else entirely. It was the size of a cricket ball, though perhaps a little bigger, if not somewhat smaller. As for the colour, you might call it grey, but you could just as accurately call it blue or orange or yellow or black, and you'd be just as wrong. There was nothing about it one could pin down. The thing, whatever it was, crackled and hissed as it hovered in mid-air between the electromagnetic towers of the Aetheric Shield Generator. It defied all powers of description and left everyone quite exhausted just looking at it.

Ben smiled at some of the nauseous expressions in the crowd. 'Staring at the Aethersphere, my friends, is the quickest route to a headache that I know of. Our human brains weren't built to process this kind of thing, and my strong advice to you all is to look elsewhere.'

From another compartment in the box he extracted a glass test tube containing a translucent golden liquid. He held it up so that the light shone through the liquid and everyone could witness its beauty. Now here was a far more pleasurable focus for the eyes.

'Particles of pure gold, suspended in solution,' Ben announced to murmurs of delight. He uncorked the tube and, crouching down, he held its rim just above the strange hovering shape. 'I'm now going to pour the gold through the Aethersphere, and you will bear witness to what happens.'

Ben remained poised in that position for a long moment, and Arabella felt herself growing tense with anticipation. She guessed that if Ben had been able to conjure a drum roll, he would have done so then. In truth, there was more than a touch of the theatrical in his sales technique.

Finally, the angle of the test tube began moving closer to horizontal. The golden liquid rolled along the glass wall of the tube and, for a second or less, it hung as a droplet at the rim. Then it fell in a thin, shining stream through the mysterious shape and into the little hole in the surface of the cube beneath.

In the tiny instant when the drop of liquid was dangling from the rim, about to fall, Arabella felt sure she saw a golden strand of it pouring out of the bottom of the shape and into the hole. The gold appeared to reach its destination *before* it had been poured! Had the Aethersphere 'predicted' the fall of the liquid? Did it *know* what was about to happen? Or had she imagined it?

These fascinating speculations were quickly swept aside as she, and everyone else, witnessed what happened next.

Ben was crouching by the device, right in front of the miniature bronze cannon that poked out of its side. As the last of the test tube's contents was poured through the Aethersphere and into the rosewood cube, there came a deep gurgling sound from within the device. Then, from out of the cannon's mouth there flared a fine white spray – like bubbles of champagne, Arabella thought. The spray covered Ben from head to foot, making him glitter and sparkle like some kind of human diamond.

Ben rose to his feet, still sparkling. He took a step or two closer to the awestruck crowd, and they backed off, suddenly fearful. Arabella stayed where she was, but was hauled back by the nervous guard, who still had his hand clamped tightly around her arm.

The glitter and sparkle faded, and Ben stood there before them, looking mildly amused by their reaction.

'I'm now protected by the Aetheric Shield,' he announced. 'Would anyone care to shoot me?'

Odin took a pistol from a holster in his belt and aimed it at Ben's forehead.

'Go ahead,' shrugged Ben.

The Sky Magister laughed and pulled the trigger.

The pistol fired.

Ben didn't move. He didn't even blink.

Everyone gasped. 'Where did the bullet go?' demanded Odin. And then he saw it – travelling at about an inch an hour towards Ben's unruffled brow.

Ben plucked the bullet from the air and handed it to Odin. 'Your bullet, sir,' he said.

Odin laughed again – it was a ragged, stuttering sort of whoop, like a man who'd just won a fortune in the casino and couldn't believe his luck.

'Shoot the boy!' he yelled at his men. 'Give him all you've got! Empty your magazines!'

Several of the guards stepped forward, raised their rapid-repeating volley guns to their shoulders and took aim at Ben.

Arabella quietly gasped. Surely that little tubeful of gold wouldn't be enough to shield the boy from such an onslaught of modern artillery? Yet the target of the guns didn't seem perturbed in the slightest. 'Come on now, don't be shy,' he urged them.

In the next instant, the air was filled with a deafening cacophony of gunfire. Everyone shook. Everyone shut their eyes in fright.

Everyone, that is, except Ben Forrester.

There he stood, as calm as ever, at the centre of the storm, while the air around him shook. The air became speckled with dozens of steel bullets, all converging at a snail's pace on his face, chest and stomach. With a casual sweep of his arm he cast them all aside, and they fell with a clatter to the wooden floorboards.

Odin came closer. This time he plucked a knife from his belt, the same one he'd threatened Arabella with earlier. He raised his arm, drawing the knife high above his head, then suddenly plunged it towards Ben's chest. The point stopped with a jerk, about five inches from its target, causing Odin to recoil painfully. He let go of the knife and massaged his sore shoulder. The knife remained in the air, moving extremely slowly towards Ben's chest. Ben took it by its handle and handed it back to Odin. After returning the knife to his belt, Odin tentatively reached out towards Ben and touched the part of his chest that he had been aiming at.

'I can touch you,' he said, surprised.

'The Aetheric Shield senses you mean no harm,' explained Ben.

'It's intelligent, then?' The Sky Magister frowned.

Ben shook his head. 'Not exactly. It's sensitive to our energies. When it picks up negative energy – when it senses that you wish to hurt me – it activates itself.'

Odin's eyes suddenly filled with alarm. 'Then nothing can hurt you?'

Ben smiled. 'Relax, Sky Magister. I'm not here to threaten you. Remember, I'm a salesman. My only business is business. So, what do you say? Are you interested in my product?'

Odin nodded. 'But I don't want the shield for myself.' He glanced around him. 'My people love me. Why should I need protection from them? I have another use in mind for your device. Your timing is good, American. In one and a half days, HMAS *Nelson* will cross the English Channel. *Horus*, my Dread Eagle, will capture it, and I want him protected by the Aetheric Shield.'

'Your Dread Eagle?' inquired Ben.

'A steel bird of prey,' explained Odin, 'twenty yards from beak to tail, with a wingspan of fifty yards. Can you protect it?'

Ben whistled. 'That sounds like a mighty big bird. I don't think I can help you, sir. Not with a machine of this size. And definitely not in one and a half days.'

Odin nodded again. 'I see.' Then he walked over to Arabella. She shivered in his ice-cold glare. He moved behind her and abruptly grabbed her in a painful neck lock. Once again she felt the blade of his knife against her neck. She struggled, but could do nothing to free herself. His breath was a loud rasp in her ear.

'Let's put it this way,' said Odin. 'You build a shield for my bird by dawn on the 18th of July, or your friend here dies. Does that sound like a fair price, Mr Salesman?'

Ben frowned. 'I usually like to deal in dollars and cents, sir. Not lives.'

'Well, let's just say we do things a little differently up here on Taranis,' murmured Odin. 'See, I'm the law in this city. And when I ask for something, nobody tells me they can't do it.'

'Then I'll do my best, sir,' said Ben, nodding meekly. 'But I will need to ask for one thing in return.'

'And what might that be?' growled Odin.

Ben drew a pistol from his belt – the same long-barrelled, ornately decorated one he'd once pointed at Arabella. This time he took aim at the Aetheric Shield Generator. 'That you let my friend go,' he said quietly.

'You overestimate the value of your product, American,' Odin chuckled. 'Your shield would be a nice addition to my defences, but my attack will go ahead, with or without it. Destroy it if you wish – it means little to me. But if you do, you'll lose any bargaining power you may still have over this lady.'

Ben raised his pistol higher so that it was now pointing at one of the enormous spinning propellers high above them – propellers that, together, kept Taranis afloat.

A ripple of alarm spread through the watching crowd. Arabella felt a muscle flinch in Odin's forearm.

The guards raised their guns once more.

'Shoot me,' Ben encouraged them. Turning to Odin, he said: 'Let her go, sir. I can do a lot of damage to your city before my shield…' He stopped and bit his lip.

'Before your shield *what*?' said Odin. 'Fades?'

He pushed Arabella aside and suddenly flung his knife hard at Ben. The blade flashed as it spun through the air. Ben ducked, and the knife flew a mere inch above his head, before clanging off a smokestack behind him and sticking in the floor.

Odin smirked. 'I rather suspected that thimbleful of golden juice wouldn't keep you protected for long.'

There came a volley of clicks as the guards got ready to shoot Ben.

'Stop!' ordered Odin. 'The lad won't cause any more trouble now he's unprotected. Besides, I want him to build a shield for my eagle. As for the girl, send her to Commodus Bane. If we feel our American friend is slacking, we can always pipe the sound of her cries into his workshop. That should convince him to work harder.'

Powerful hands grabbed Arabella and began marching her at a brisk pace towards a doorway. The guards were about to haul her through it when Ben said: 'I'll need her with me.'

'What?' came Odin's impatient cry.

'She helped me create the Aetheric Shield Generator,' Ben told him. 'Without her, it'll be impossible.'

Arabella wondered what game Ben was playing. Why did he even care about saving her?

Odin sighed. 'OK, you can have her.'

As she was led back out onto the terrace, she sensed Ben smiling at her but refused to look at him, still furious with him for what he had agreed to do.

'I'll also need gold to fuel the generator,' said Ben. 'As much as you can give me.'

'Of course,' agreed the Sky Magister. 'We have storerooms full of the stuff.'

'And Miles,' added Ben.

'Miles? Miles of what?'

'Just Miles. He's an automaton belonging to Lady Arabella. I'd say he proved himself pretty darn indispensable during the development of the generator, wouldn't you agree, ma'am?'

She found herself nodding. 'He's – he's in the luggage compartment of my air carriage,' she said.

Five minutes later, Ben and Arabella were escorted through the doorway into the interior of Taranis. Behind them, guards carried boxes containing Miles and the Aetheric Shield machine. Odin's parting shot rang in their ears: 'That shield will be ready in time for the *Nelson*, or I swear it'll be death for both of you.'

PART III

17 JULY 1845

CHAPTER SEVENTEEN

THE NEXT MORNING

A beam of bright silver light, shining through a knothole in a wooden wall, struck Arabella's left eyelid. She blinked, and awoke. With a sigh, she remembered where she was – imprisoned on Taranis. Her limbs ached and her skin prickled after a night spent on a thin bed of straw. Massaging her arms, she struggled into a sitting position and leaned back against the rough wall of the wooden cell that since yesterday evening had served as her home.

For someone who craved the freedom of the skies, being locked in a windowless wooden cell was frustrating to say the least. The cell had two rooms: a bedchamber and a tiny bathrooom. Apart from the thin shafts of exterior light coming through the knotholes, the only illumination came from a tiny gas lamp on a table by the door. The door was locked and bolted from the outside, and the shuffling sounds coming from the corridor beyond may have been rats but were more likely guards, so any escape plans would have to be put on hold for now.

Even if she managed to escape, Arabella probably wouldn't get very far, since she didn't have the first idea where she was. The journey here from the roof terrace yesterday evening had been long and complex, with so many twists and turns that she'd rapidly lost all sense of direction. Taranis, on the inside, turned out to be an endless, gloomy warren of lopsided corridors and rickety staircases. However, to judge from the number of staircases they had descended, she guessed she was on one of the lower tiers.

On their way here they'd passed hundreds of people, all pale and malnourished and dressed in the same drab blue overalls. Some had been carrying trays of food or baskets of laundry; others had been on their knees or up ladders, repairing walls, pipes and gas lights. Arabella assumed they must be slaves from captured vessels. Through open doorways off some of the corridors, she'd glimpsed rooms filled with fine furniture, tapestries, gilt-framed paintings and gleaming trinkets. It was easy to see why Sky Magister Odin was popular – he had provided the Taranites with more stolen goods than they knew what to do with, not to mention a continuous supply of free labour.

Arabella had no idea where Ben was. He'd been escorted to another cell, she assumed, and at some point they'd probably be summoned to a workshop and told to get on with building an Aetheric Shield for the Dread Eagle. She, of course, would refuse to do any such thing. They could threaten her with torture and starvation and whatever they liked. There was no way that she, Lady Arabella West, was going to help build anything that would threaten her compatriots.

Speaking of starvation, she hoped they would be serving breakfast soon. The meal they'd delivered to her cell the night before had been a watery stew with a few lumps of fatty meat and vegetables floating around in it. If the Taranites wanted to get any work out of their slaves, the least they could do was to serve up some decent fare.

With a yawn and a stretch, Arabella got to her feet and went to the bathroom. She got dressed in the blue overalls they'd given her – the slave uniform. Her original clothes, along with her aethercell – her only chance of communicating with the outside world – had been taken from her.

Thanks to Ben's insistence, at least they'd left her with Miles. She crossed to the far corner of the room and opened the box containing the Logical Englishman. She stood him on his feet and

switched him on. It was a comfort to see those eyes of
his come to life – strange how much one could miss
a machine.

'Hello Miles.'

'Greetings, my lady. Where are we?'

'We're on board a floating city somewhere over the
Channel, being held prisoner by a sky pirate named
Odin. He's the fellow responsible for all those airship
disappearances recently. He's been capturing them
with this enormous metal bird he calls his Dread
Eagle. And no one's spotted him yet because he hides
his city inside a cloud.'

'I see,' said Miles, taking all of this in with admirable
calmness.

'And that American mercenary, Mr Forrester, has
shown up again,' Arabella added. 'He's brought a
working Aetheric Shield Generator with him, which
he wants to sell to Odin, and now Odin wants Mr
Forrester, you and me to build him a shield for his
Dread Eagle. He wants it in one and a half days –
well, one day now – so he can use the Dread Eagle to
capture HMAS *Nelson*. If we don't oblige him, he says
he'll kill us.'

She observed a flickering of the yellow light in
Miles's eyes as he processed all this information. Then
he asked: 'Why does Odin think we can help Mr
Forrester build an Aetheric Shield?'

'Because Mr Forrester told him that we had assisted
him in building the generator and that he needed us

with him. I'm not sure why he said that – it may have been to save me from torture.'

Miles did some more heavy processing, finishing with a worried puff of steam from the exhaust pipe in his hat.

'Were you threatened with *torture*, my lady?'

'Yes, at the hands of a most unpleasant-sounding chap by the name of Commodus Bane.'

'I calculate that our situation is most precarious,' announced Miles.

'I had a feeling you might say that,' said Arabella, feeling oddly cheered by his words. 'So tell me in numbers – I know you love your numbers, Miles! – what are our chances?'

Machinery hissed and clanked in Miles's brain. 'I would estimate our chances to be one in seventy-five.'

'Coming from you, those are not bad numbers!'

'I fear you are not taking our plight entirely seriously, my lady.'

Arabella patted him on the head. 'You should try looking on the bright side, Miles.'

'And what bright side would that be?' enquired the Logical Englishman.

Arabella thought about this – there had to be a bright side, surely!

'Well, we're not dead,' she said eventually.

'That is true,' Miles conceded.

CHAPTER EIGHTEEN

THE DIABOLICAL PROJECT

After breakfast – which amounted to a hunk of stale bread washed down with a mug of tea – Arabella and Miles were escorted down some more crooked corridors and unsteady staircases to a vast room with bare walls and a floor heaped high with great piles of junk. Having shown them in, the guards departed the room, slamming the door behind them.

In the middle of the room, soaring majestically above the piles of scrap, stood *Horus*, the Dread Eagle. Arabella stood near the door, stunned once again by the colossal size and ferocious grace of the steel raptor. Now that the thing was stationary, and not threatening to kill her, she was able to survey it at leisure. She studied the cruel hook of its beak, the intensity of its predatory stare, the thousands of dagger-sharp, overlapping steel feathers, and was forced to admit it had a terrifying beauty.

'Impressive, huh?' called Ben from the far side of the room. He emerged from behind one of the mounds of scrap, clutching an odd assortment of metal pieces. He came over and laid them down on a workbench, then wiped his hands on a piece of cloth.

'Morning, ma'am. I trust you slept well? And Miles – well, what do you know, the old gang's back together! Miles, I think we may be desirous of your expertise when it comes to some of the more technical aspects of this project.' He nodded towards the bird. 'As you can see, we've been set quite a tall order.'

'Miles and I will not be assisting you in your treacherous activities,' said Arabella stiffly.

'I'm sorry to hear that,' said Ben, looking a little crestfallen, 'especially after I rescued you from Commodus Bane.'

'I would prefer to face ten Commodus Banes than spend a minute helping you sabotage my country's war effort. Was it not enough that you denied Britain access to this technology? Did you then have to sell it to an unsavoury pirate like Odin? Have you no morals, Mr Forrester? You're an American, aren't you? You're supposed to be our ally. Where is your sense of loyalty?'

Ben's response was to turn his back on her and continue with his work. He began sorting through his pieces of scrap metal, holding each one up in turn and examining it closely before discarding it. 'I'm an American, sure,' he muttered as he worked. 'But unlike my government, I don't pick sides in this war. The only loyalty I have is to myself. In the end that's the only cause worth fighting for.'

Arabella was left speechless. Clearly there could be no meeting of minds with this young man. They were worlds apart, and it was just her rotten luck that she'd been landed with him as her only potential ally against Odin.

She tried one final approach: 'Surely you must realise that Odin plans to kill you as soon as you've delivered him the shield. There can be no *profit*' – she wrinkled her nose in distaste at the word – 'for you in remaining here. Why don't we pool our resources and try to escape?'

Ben spat on a piece of metal and rubbed it with his sleeve, then inspected the result. 'You escape if you want to,' he said without looking up. 'But don't concern yourself with me. I've met Odin's type before. He likes to play hardball, but he's basically okay. We can do business.'

The boy was oddly trusting, even naïve, for someone so cynical. He was as enigmatic in his attitude towards Odin as he was in his attitude towards *her*.

'If business is all you care about,' she asked, 'then why did you lie to Odin about me and Miles helping you with the shield?'

Ben looked up. 'I honestly don't know what came over me,' he said with a mysterious smile. 'Perhaps I'm going soft.'

As she watched him go back to work, Arabella heard a soft clicking sound at her left elbow, the mechanical equivalent of a clearing of the throat. 'My lady,' said Miles. 'If I might make so bold, do you not think it would be a good idea to assist young Mr Forrester in building the Aetheric Shield – or at least go through the motions of doing so – until we can work out some positive plan of action.'

'Why might that be a good idea?' Arabella asked him sternly.

'To encourage the Taranites to believe that you are co-operating.'

Arabella stared at Miles for a moment, then at the giant bird. She imagined that beak, those talons, swooping down on the *Nelson*.

'No!' she said. 'No! No! No!' And she turned and banged on the workshop door.

The lock clicked and the door opened. A guard poked his head in. 'What do you want?'

'Do as you wish with me,' declared Arabella, 'but, as an Englishwoman, I will not be party to this diabolical project.'

The guard looked dumbly at her for a moment before muttering something into the battered aethercell attached to the collar of his jacket. A few minutes later, Arabella heard heavy footsteps approaching along the corridor. A much bigger, meaner-looking guard appeared in the doorway. His fat, bald head protruded from his muscular shoulders with no sign of a neck. In his giant pink hands he carried a pair of heavy iron bracelets, which he violently slammed closed over Arabella's wrists.

'Come with me!' he ordered, and, without waiting for her to obey him, he pulled her out of the room.

'My lady…!' she heard Miles call. Then the door banged shut behind her, and she was being dragged along the corridor.

They descended more staircases. The deeper they went, the lower the ceilings became, until Arabella had to crouch to avoid hitting her head. It seemed that these lower floors – the oldest parts of Taranis – were slowly being crushed by the weight of new floors being added above. Indeed, she couldn't help noticing the deep cracks in many of the dark, ancient-looking wooden pillars.

They had gone so deep that Arabella was sure they must now be inside the giant metal bowl beneath the city. The light was so dim here, she nearly lost her footing on a couple of occasions. Each time, the burly guard pulled her roughly to her feet and dragged her onwards. Echoing in the distance, but getting ever louder, she could hear sounds of people in pain – crying, sobbing and groaning.

Eventually, at the bottom of perhaps the twentieth set of stairs, they arrived in front of a heavy oak door with an iron grille set in the middle of it. There was no doubt that the sounds of distress were coming from the other side of this door. For the first time, her escort grinned, revealing his broken yellow Taranite teeth and making Arabella almost faint from the warm stench of rotten meat that flowed from between his swollen lips.

'Welcome,' he said, 'to the lair of Commodus Bane.'

CHAPTER NINETEEN

THE TORTURE CHAMBER

rabella had suspected that this was to be her destination, but hearing it confirmed sent a cool jangle of fear through her.

The guard selected a key from a chain hanging from his belt and unlocked the door. She remembered the chant from yesterday:

Commodus Bane, the man is insane...

Beyond lay a long, dim corridor lined with iron-barred cells. As they advanced along it, she couldn't help glancing into the murky interiors of the cells, where she saw pale, thin-limbed figures with bright eyes starting from their bony faces. Their moans and whimpers thudded against her ears, and her knees grew weak from the effort of walking.

Commodus Bane, he knows about pain!

Perhaps she should have listened to Miles and pretended to co-operate, then waited for an opportunity to escape. She had been mad to rebel openly. Did she want to end up like one of these wretches in the cells? The Taranites didn't care that she was a person of noble rank, daughter of the great Lord Alfred West. To them she was like any other slave, to be worked to death, tortured or killed at their pleasure.

At the far end of the corridor another door creaked on its hinges and Arabella felt herself being shoved forward. The guard pushed her with such force that she lost her balance and fell to her knees on a hard stone floor. Behind her the door slammed shut.

She was in a dungeon of some kind, so big and dark, she couldn't see its furthest corners. At one end was a roaring fire. Standing next to the fire was a thin man in a long black cloak and a tall stovepipe hat. He had his back to her. As she waited there on the cold floor, a faint, rhythmic hissing sound came to her ears. Was it his breathing?

After a while the man turned to face her. The lower part of his face was hidden by a leather mask, with a thin slit for his mouth. His eyes were covered by a pair of gold-rimmed, dark-lensed goggles that flickered and shone in the light of the fire. With so much of his face concealed, Arabella could get no sense of the man or his state of mind. But his stance – still and erect, hands behind his back, head tilted slightly forward – spoke to her of someone calm, focused and infinitely patient.

He began moving very slowly towards her. The approach of this masked, goggled figure was so unnerving that she had to suppress a desire to shrink into a corner.

When he was very close, the man stopped and looked down at her. The hissing was louder, but it didn't seem like breathing now, more like machinery. She could feel the thump of her heart, banging in time with the hiss. His arms appeared from beneath the folds of his cloak and she saw that the left one gleamed like metal. That hissing sound, she now understood, was the movement of his steel fingers as they continually opened, then closed into a fist, then opened again. He glanced up at something behind her. Before she could turn to see what it was, an invisible hand grabbed her and raised her to her feet, and she realised that her giant escort was still here – he'd been standing behind her all the time.

The guard hauled her to a table near the fire. He picked her up as though she were a bale of straw and placed her on it. She tried to resist, but he was too strong. She felt her ankles being tied tightly to the legs of the table. The rough rope burned her skin. Then the bracelets were removed and her arms were yanked above her head, and she felt the same rope pinioning her wrists to the other two table legs.

Arabella tried to keep her breathing even – tried not to think of her helplessness or allow herself to slip into panic. The hiss of the thin man's steam-driven arm grew louder. He passed the table where Arabella lay and went over to the fire. The hissing stopped. Leaning forward, the man placed the tip of his steel forefinger in the flames. She watched, horrified, as the finger gradually turned pale pink, then rose, then orange.

'You may have heard of me,' said the man as he watched his finger glowing in the fire. 'I am Doctor Commodus Bane.' Hearing him speak was a shock. From what she had heard of him, Arabella had assumed he must be a brute – little more than an animal – but he had the voice of an educated man.

He approached the table, a wisp of smoke rising from his index finger, which now blushed a deep cherry-red.

'Find the centres of maximum pain,' he said. 'That's where the heart lies. That's where the truth lies. So Allenson once told me.'

He looked down at Arabella through the cold blackness of his goggles. She glimpsed moist, thin lips through the slit in the mask.

'What do you want?' she managed to whisper.

'What do I want?' he echoed. 'I want what I always want – to enjoy myself. And I will. But that's beside the point. We're here to find out what *you* want, Lady Arabella West.'

He raised his steel arm, and she could feel the heat from it on her cheek.

'Why did you come here?' he whispered close to her ear. 'What is it that you want? The Sky Magister wants his shield; that's all he's interested in. He wants me to persuade you to get back into that workshop and help Mr Forrester. And I can do that – of course I can. I have some highly persuasive tools at my disposal.'

The glowing tip of his superheated finger danced above her face – a reminder she hardly needed of one of those 'persuasive tools'.

'But I'm not interested in forcing you to perform a role. That's too easy! Any animal trainer worth his salt can do that. I'm interested in *you*, young lady. What motivates you? I can't help it. I have a curious nature... I'm going to ask you some questions. And I want you to tell me the truth. If you tell me the truth, then I promise nothing bad will happen to you... But if you lie to me, you should know that I will burn you.'

'How can you know...' Arabella swallowed. 'How can you know whether I'm telling the truth or lying?'

Bane emitted a sudden high-pitched giggle. 'You forget I have some experience in these matters. Many people have lain where you are now, looking up at me, their eyes full of hope and despair. Hope and despair, Lady Arabella. Always try to maintain a balance between these two – that's what Allenson taught me. Too much of one or the other is never good. But when I get the balance right, they all become very helpful.

They answer my questions. Some lie, some tell the truth. After a while, you learn to tell the difference… So let's see how you do, shall we? Will you tell me the truth… or will you burn?'

She could feel his other hand stroking her hair.

'We'll start with an easy one, shall we? What are you? Are you a performer in a flying circus as you told us – or are you a scientist who helped build an invisible shield, as your friend Mr Forrester claims?'

Arabella couldn't take her eyes off the red-hot fingertip as it swayed hypnotically through the darkness just above her face. She forced herself to think. If she said she was a scientist, she'd then be faced with the impossible task of explaining her arrival here in an armed air carriage with a state-of-the-art automaton on board. If she said she was a flying-circus performer, she'd still face awkward explanations, and they'd have no further reason to keep her alive. Neither option was good. She had to say…

'Both. I – I'm both.'

Again he made that childish giggle. 'An aerial artiste *and* a top scientist – and at such a young age! It would be impressive – if it were true. But you'll forgive me if I have my doubts…'

'You can believe whatever you wish,' she said quickly. 'It's the truth.'

She felt a rush of heat and painful brightness as the scorching digit darted close to her eye.

He was going to blind her!

A memory came to her then of the many Taranites she'd seen wearing eyepatches – were they all victims of Commodus Bane?

She felt his human hand on her arm where it lay tethered above her head. He was pushing up the sleeve of her overall, as the burning finger moved north, away from her face. The heat became intense in a spot on the pale, tender underside of her forearm, just below the wrist.

'Tell me the truth,' he breathed, 'if you want to preserve your perfect skin.'

Arabella gritted her teeth and thought of her father, and the British flag, and Heroes' Day with the Waterloo veterans saluting as they marched past the Cenotaph...

'I *have* told you the truth!' she screamed, and a second later her world dissolved into bright, jagged colours of pain.

CHAPTER TWENTY

THE WORM OF DOUBT

Arabella must have passed out, for the next thing she was aware of was awakening to find herself still strapped to the table. Her arm was screaming at her in hot, throbbing waves. Her vision swam with shadows and the gleam of reflected firelight. Blinking away the tears, she saw, with a tightening in her heart, that Bane was still there – the twin black circles of his goggles, like insect eyes, studying her. In his human hand he was holding up the daguerreotype of her father. She moaned when she saw this, and pulled with all her might at her restraints, but the flexing of her muscles only intensified the pain in her arm.

'So you're the daughter of Lord Alfred West,' he said. 'I should have guessed. You're a spy, just like your father. You want to be a hero to your country, like he was. You want to be brave, to live up to his memory. I understand. But you don't have to worry. You have nothing to live up to, Lady Arabella. You see, your father was not who you think he was.'

'What – what are you talking about?' gasped Arabella.

'Ah, then you don't know.' Bane chuckled. 'Well, that shouldn't surprise me. Not many people do. Allenson knew, but only because he was part of the same conspiracy. Your father, my dear, was a spy for the French!'

'*No!*' Arabella screamed

'Lord West was a traitor,' Bane continued in a singsong voice. 'He wasn't killed by French assassins, as the story went – he killed *himself* to avoid the shame of exposure. The affair was covered up, and his reputation kept intact. Anything else would have been far too embarrassing for the British government.'

'You're a liar!'

'I expose lies, I don't tell them,' said Bane smoothly. He held his metal finger, now a smoky purple, to the daguerreotype, and Arabella had to watch her father's face start to smoulder.

'Say goodbye to the man you thought you knew,' murmured Bane.

Her tears started welling up again as the image of her beloved father gradually warped and turned to black.

There was a knock at the door. It creaked open and there followed an exchange of hurried, urgent words. After a nod from Commodus Bane, the guard began untying Arabella.

'It appears,' said Bane, 'that Mr Forrester and your automaton have gone on strike. They claim they're unable to work without your help, so the Sky Magister has ordered me to send you back. Well, so it goes. I've enjoyed meeting you, Lady Arabella. It's been an interesting session, wouldn't you agree? And an enlightening one – for both of us. We must arrange a follow-up. Now we know for certain you're a spy, you'll need to tell me all about the proposed route of HMAS *Nelson* across the Channel. But first things first.'

She felt the iron bracelets click back onto her wrists as the guard hauled her off the table. '*Au revoir,*' said Bane. 'See you soon.' As she left the room, she heard him laugh: 'Don't be a stranger now. Come back any time. You know I'll make you welcome!'

Arabella trudged the long flights of steps back up to the workshop in a daze of pain and bewilderment. Her arm still stung horribly from the touch of Commodus Bane's finger, and there was a fierce red mark there that she knew would soon become an ugly scar. But the misery and confusion that reigned inside her head

at Bane's accusations about her father were far worse
than any physical pain he'd inflicted. Of course she
didn't believe a word the man had said. Her father was
a hero, and a sadistic monster like Commodus Bane
could never make her believe otherwise. Nevertheless,
the ogre had very cleverly planted a worm in her
brain, and she knew she would never be able to think
of her father again without that little worm whispering
its doubts. She would now have to make it her
personal quest to look into these allegations and prove
beyond suspicion that her father was the shining hero
and loyal servant of Britain she'd always believed
him to be.

When they finally arrived at the workshop, the
guard relieved Arabella of her manacles and pushed
her through the door. She fell in a heap, thoroughly
exhausted after her ordeal and the long climb that
followed it. Ben Forrester ran forward and helped
her to her feet. For all her misgivings about the boy,
she had to admit it gave her some pleasure to see him.
Then again, after Commodus Bane, Napoleon himself
would probably have made a welcome sight!

CHAPTER TWENTY-ONE

THE FRENCH GIRL

The boy seemed concerned with her health, which was an agreeable surprise. 'Ma'am, you don't look too hot!' he declared, helping her to a chair. As she gratefully took a seat, Miles came trundling up and handed her a chipped mug filled with water. His gentleman's attire had been swapped for a set of 'prisoner blue' overalls – the little exhaust chimney no longer poked out of a top hat, but a peaked cap.

'My lady, how are you feeling?' he asked.

'I've had better days, Miles,' she said after taking a long, refreshing gulp. 'But I've survived a session with Commodus Bane with, I believe, most of my dignity intact. I don't know how many could say that.'

'You're a brave gal and no mistake,' smiled Ben.

Arabella nodded graciously at the compliment. 'And I must thank you both for your solidarity,' she said. 'If you hadn't downed tools, I'm sure I'd still be strapped to Dr Bane's torture table.'

'It was the least we could do,' Ben mumbled. She was surprised to see him blush, and wondered what could be bothering him. Eventually, after several false starts, he came out with it. 'Hell, if I was half the man I like to think I am, I'd have come down there and tried to rescue you.'

'And what good would that have done anybody?' said Arabella in what she hoped was a reassuring tone. 'Those guards would have caught and killed you in five minutes flat, and I'd be no better off. Tell him, Miles. Hit him with some your numbers.'

'Mr Forrester and I have already had this conversation, my lady – several times – and I assured him on each occasion that his plan had approximately nought point nought nought nought one per cent probability of success.'

'There you are then!' said Arabella, fixing Ben with a triumphant look. 'Wouldn't you agree, Mr Forrester, now that you've been made aware of the savagery of this place, that a far better use for your energies would be to help Miles and me devise an escape plan?'

Ben pursed his lips, then shook his head. 'The savagery comes as no surprise, ma'am. But a good salesman refrains from casting moral judgement on his customers. Of course I am upset that you suffered ill-treatment from these people, but if you're honest, you'll admit that you brought that on yourself. You could have played along like your wise friend Miles here suggested, and no one would have got hurt.' He reached into the inside pocket of his jacket and pulled out some folded sheets of paper. 'I now have a monetary contract with Sky Magister Odin, signed this morning, to build an Aetheric Shield for his eagle, and it is my intention to fulfill that contract to the best of my ability. So, if you don't mind, I'm going to need to get back to work.'

It saddened Arabella to hear this – she thought she'd noticed signs of a more enlightened perspective in Ben, but clearly he remained as convinced as ever that the pursuit of money was the worthiest goal to which a man could aspire. She watched Ben and Miles move to a corner of the room near the workbench, where a large metal cabinet had been placed on its back. Ben donned a pair of welding goggles that reminded her for an uncomfortable moment of Bane. He fired up a carbon arc-welding torch, while Miles picked up a length of metal tubing and gripped it in a clamp that he had fitted in place of his left hand. The automaton placed one end of the tubing against the side of the metal cabinet, then Ben aimed his torch at the meeting point of the two objects and began to weld them together.

Arabella sat there for a long time, observing the two of them as they constructed a scaled-up version of the original Aetheric Shield Generator. She felt weak inside, and so hungry. Her arm still hurt terribly, and her mind kept flashing up horrid images of Bane's glowing finger hovering near her eye. It was rare for her to feel this way, but she honestly didn't know what to do next.

Lunch was eventually served, which turned out to be a combination of breakfast and supper: more watery stew accompanied by a hunk of stale bread. It was food that even yesterday she would have turned her nose up at, yet she eyed it now as she might a royal banquet. Ben, who must have been equally hungry, finished his a lot quicker, and was soon back at his workbench.

As she chewed on a chunk of stringy meat, Arabella watched Ben wrapping a copper wire tightly around a long bar of iron. To Miles, he said: 'I figure if we can increase the current, and use more turns of copper wire around this soft iron core, that should make the electromagnets a lot stronger.'

'A bigger current will mean more heat, sir' replied Miles, 'which could end up melting the wire. It would be better to increase the strength simply by adding more turns.'

Ben craned his neck to look up at the bird. 'I think we'll have to take the risk and do both, my friend.'

He walked over to the door and knocked on it. The guard put his head in. 'We need more copper wire,' said Ben.

A few minutes later a slave girl in prisoner-blue overalls walked in, carrying a large roll of copper wire. She looked about sixteen, Arabella thought, and strikingly thin. As she headed back out of the room, the girl glanced over at Arabella's food. Arabella was still achingly hungry and looking forward to finishing it, but the girl looked as though she needed it a lot more. Arabella beckoned to her, and the girl came over.

'Would you like some?' she offered, holding out the remains of the stew and the crust of bread.

The girl glanced worriedly over her shoulder towards the door where the guard was standing just out of sight.

'It's OK,' coaxed Arabella. 'I won't tell.'

The girl took the bowl, sat down on the floor and began scooping up the stew hungrily. 'I haven't eaten since two days,' she said between mouthfuls, in a strong French accent. When the bowl was entirely clean of stew, she turned to the bread crust, devouring it in seconds.

'Thank you for your kindness,' she said when she'd finished. 'My name is Marie Daguerre. I was a passenger on the aircruiser *La Fayette*, travelling with my aunt. We were captured four weeks ago. My aunt died yesterday, and I'm afraid I will also die soon. They have so many slaves now, since they caught the

Borealis, they don't even bother feeding us. There are always more to replace us. They will work us until we drop, then throw us off the edge of the city. Are you from the *Borealis*? The same thing will happen to you, I'm afraid.'

All this came out in a nervous torrent, while the girl kept checking over her shoulder for the reappearance of the guard.

'I'm not from the *Borealis*,' Arabella replied. 'I'm an aviatrix. My name is Arabella. My air carriage was captured yesterday.'

The girl glanced up at the Dread Eagle that towered above their heads. 'I hate that thing,' she shuddered. 'What are you doing here?' She nodded towards Ben and Miles. 'What are *they* doing?'

'We're being forced to build a shield for that monster,' said Arabella, 'so that it can attack a powerful British battlecruiser.'

Marie's eyes became wide. 'What battlecruiser?'

Arabella studied the girl. Ordinarily she would regard a French girl as her enemy, but here on Taranis they were, she supposed, temporary allies against a common threat. Besides, the girl was probably dying, so what did it matter?

'HMAS *Nelson*,' she whispered, 'flagship of the Royal Air Fleet. It's due to cross the Channel tomorrow morning. The pirates want to capture it.'

Marie stared at her, astonished.

'But I won't let it happen,' said Arabella, sounding a lot more certain than she felt. 'Somehow I've got to stop it, I just don't know how yet.'

The French girl glanced behind her once again, then edged closer to Arabella, leaning in towards her ear. 'Maybe I can help you,' she whispered. 'I have – I have seen something…'

'Oi!' came a sudden shout from behind them, making them both jump. The guard had entered the room behind them and he was now glaring at Marie. 'You know the rules, girl,' he bellowed. 'No fraternising with other prisoners. Now get out of here!' He marched over and pulled her up. As he dragged her from the room, Marie turned her head and mouthed something at Arabella, but she was at a loss to understand what it was.

CHAPTER TWENTY-TWO

THE FLOOR PLAN

More hours passed. Arabella watched the new generator getting closer and closer to completion. Ben and Miles erected a couple of timber scaffolding towers on either side of it, straddled by a wooden platform. On the platform they placed a large black cauldron, positioning it directly above the generator.

'We need more gold,' Ben told the door guard. 'If we're going to test this thing, we're going to need lots more gold.'

Not long afterwards, slaves began to arrive carrying crates of gold coins, rings, necklaces, bracelets and other jewellery. Arabella was disappointed that Marie was not among them.

Ben put on a cloth face mask, grabbed a crate of gold trinkets and climbed one of the wooden towers. He removed the lid from the black cauldron and Arabella saw fumes spilling out into the air. She caught a whiff of something sharp and bitter, and it made her cough. Ben quickly poured the gold pieces into the cauldron, then closed the lid.

'Would you be so kind as to pass me another crate, ma'am?' he asked Arabella. 'I fear Miles lacks the height to be of much help in this instance.'

Arabella had decidedly mixed feelings about assisting him, but decided in the end it would be churlish not to. She went over to the pile of crates and picked one up, staggering a little under its surprising weight. The gleaming yellow objects in the crate were so pretty, it seemed sad to destroy them, especially for such a cause.

'Whenever you're ready, your ladyship,' said Ben, a touch impatiently.

'Sorry,' she said, passing it up to him.

She watched him pour the gold into the cauldron; this time she had the presence of mind to cover her nose and mouth.

'What is that stuff in there?' she asked.

'Nitro-hydrochloric acid,' said Ben, as he closed the lid again. 'It'll dissolve the gold – turn it into chloroauric acid. Then we'll add a little sodium citrate solution and, hey presto! we get our gold particles – the fuel for the shield.'

As she was passing the next crate to him, her eye was caught by a dainty little gold jar half-submerged in a pile of coins. Peeping out of the jar was a rolled-up piece of paper. Putting down the crate, she plucked out the paper and unfurled it.

'I don't want to rush you, ma'am, but you know we're up against the clock here,' complained Ben.

'Hush!' she said, as she stared at the paper. Hastily scrawled upon it was a diagram. It looked like a plan, showing a maze of rooms and corridors. At the bottom was scribbled *Deuxième Etage* – 'Second Floor'.

From the desperation in the pen strokes, she was absolutely sure that this was the work of her new friend, Marie Daguerre. Marie must have drawn the plan and secreted it in the jar, hoping it would get to Arabella. The plan had to be a message. 'I have seen something,' the girl had said. She must have seen it on the second floor. Arabella read the only other words on the paper: *Usine du Nuage*. A line extended from these words to one of the rooms near the centre of the floor plan. She frowned, trying to recall her French lessons at school. *Usine* meant 'factory'; *nuage* meant 'cloud' – 'Factory of the Cloud'… 'Cloud Factory'!

Suddenly it came to her: the giant cloud that enshrouded Taranis had to have been created somehow, and in that room they would find the machine responsible! If they could disable or destroy that machine, the cloud would disappear, leaving Taranis exposed and no longer able to launch its surprise attacks. The British strike force would see the city long before it could launch its Dread Eagle.

Excitedly, she showed the paper to Miles and explained her idea. Ben crouched on his haunches on the wooden platform above them, listening closely.

Miles was almost rattling with anxiety by the time she'd finished. 'Speaking candidly, my lady, may I say that this sounds like a most reckless venture, with a vanishingly small prospect of success. Such a room is certain to be very heavily guarded. I can only assume you are intending this as a suicide mission, for I cannot imagine how you believe you can get all the way to the second floor and back without being detected. And even if you manage to gain access to the room and sabotage the machine, the likelihood is that they will have it working again within a matter of hours, rendering your self-sacrifice futile.'

'A matter of hours, Miles, might be all we need,' said Arabella. 'Don't forget, Diana and Cassie will have reported their discovery by now, and London will have been alerted. There are bound to be surveillance vessels crisscrossing the Channel as we speak, trying to find the cloud. If I can expose Taranis for even a short while, it'll be worth it.'

'Worth your death, ma'am?' commented Ben from above their heads. He gave a low, mournful whistle. 'I never will claim to understand you patriots, but I'll say one thing: your country sure is lucky to have people like you willing to lay down your lives like this.'

Arabella, excited to have rediscovered a purpose, ignored this remark. 'I'll need your help opening the door to the Cloud Factory,' she said to Miles.

The Logical Englishman emitted a resigned puff of smoke. 'Of course I will do as you ask, my lady, whatever my personal views on the matter. After all, I am here only to advise, and to serve.'

'Thank you.'

'Hey, would you two mind at least waiting until tomorrow?' Ben asked. 'Not that I expect you to succeed, but in case by some miracle you do, I'd like at least to get paid before you expose my customer to the full might of your Royal Air Fleet.'

Arabella treated him to her most contemptuous glare. 'We'll do it now,' she said.

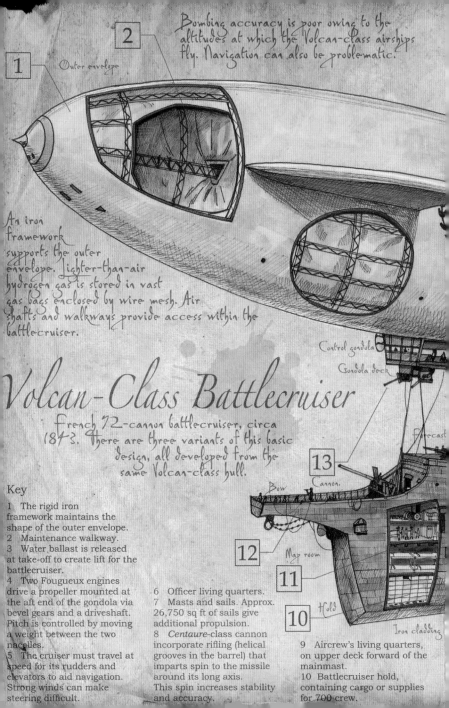

1 Outer envelope

2 Bombing accuracy is poor owing to the altitudes at which the Volcan-class airships fly. Navigation can also be problematic.

An iron framework supports the outer envelope. Lighter-than-air hydrogen gas is stored in vast gas bags enclosed by wire mesh. Air shafts and walkways provide access within the battlecruiser.

Control gondola

Gondola deck

Volcan-Class Battlecruiser

French 72-cannon battlecruiser, circa 1843. There are three variants of this basic design, all developed from the same Volcan-class hull.

Forecast

13

Bow   Cannon

Key

1   The rigid iron framework maintains the shape of the outer envelope.
2   Maintenance walkway.
3   Water ballast is released at take-off to create lift for the battlecruiser.
4   Two Fougueux engines drive a propeller mounted at the aft end of the gondola via bevel gears and a driveshaft. Pitch is controlled by moving a weight between the two nacelles.
5   The cruiser must travel at speed for its rudders and elevators to aid navigation. Strong winds can make steering difficult.

6   Officer living quarters.
7   Masts and sails. Approx. 26,750 sq ft of sails give additional propulsion.
8   *Centaure*-class cannon incorporate rifling (helical grooves in the barrel) that imparts spin to the missile around its long axis. This spin increases stability and accuracy.

12

Map room

11

Hold

10

Iron cladding

9   Aircrew's living quarters, on upper deck forward of the mainmast.
10   Battlecruiser hold, containing cargo or supplies for 700 crew.

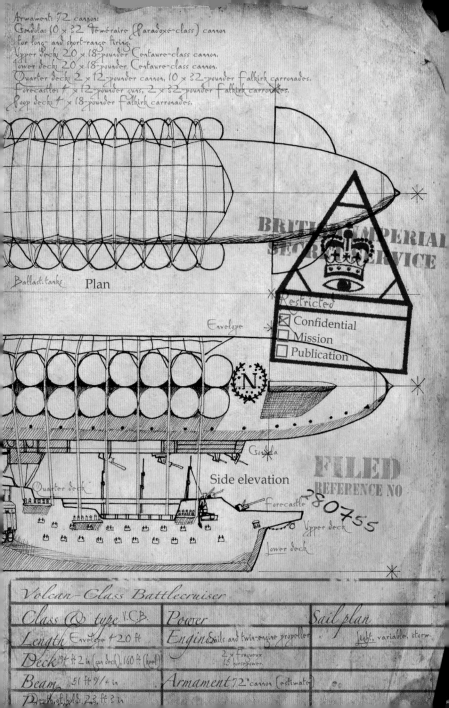

Armament: 72 cannon:
Gondola: 10 x 32 Téméraire (Paradoxé-class) cannon
for long- and short-range firing.
Upper deck: 20 x 18-pounder Centaure-class cannon.
Lower deck: 20 x 18-pounder Centaure-class cannon.
Quarter deck: 2 x 12-pounder cannon, 10 x 32-pounder Falkirk carronades.
Forecastle: 4 x 12-pounder guns, 2 x 32-pounder Falkirk carronades.
Poop deck: 4 x 18-pounder Falkirk carronades.

Ballast tanks   Plan

BRITISH IMPERIAL
SECRET SERVICE

Restricted
☒ Confidential
☐ Mission
☐ Publication

Envelope

Side elevation

Gondola

Quarter deck

Forecastle

Upper deck

Lower deck

FILED
REFERENCE NO
280755

Volcan-Class Battlecruiser		
Class & type V.C.B.	Power	Sail plan
Length Envelope 420 ft	Engine Sails and twin-engine propeller	Light, variable, storm.
Deck 191 ft 2 in (gun deck), 160 ft (keel)	2 x Fougueux 15 horsepower.	
Beam 51 ft 9 1/4 in	Armament 72 cannon (estimate)	
Depth of hold 23 ft 3 in		

420 ft long with a hydrogen capacity of 400,000 cu ft. Two 15 horsepower Fougueux engines drive a propeller mounted at the aft end of the gondola via bevel gears and a driveshaft. Pitch is controlled by moving a weight between the two nacelles.

Motto: Honneur, Patrie, Valeur, Discipline

Rigging

Propeller

Poop deck

Water-filled ballast tanks.

Propeller driven by Fougueux 15 horsepower engines.

3

4

Take-off:
Hydrogen gas makes the battlecruiser lighter than air. To take off, water ballast is released and the battlecruiser rises. Atmospheric pressure is equalised gradually as the airship rises by gently reducing the gas bag to minimise the risk of explosion.

Rudder

5

6

7

8

9

Centaure-class cannon.

11 Map room.
12 Bow.
13 *Téméraire (Paradoxe-class)* cannon for long- and short-range firing.

Volcan-Class Battlecruiser

Almost twice the size of the Tirailleur, this is one of the largest and most heavily armoured craft in the French Imperial Fleet. Its gas envelope is protected by an iron exoskeleton.

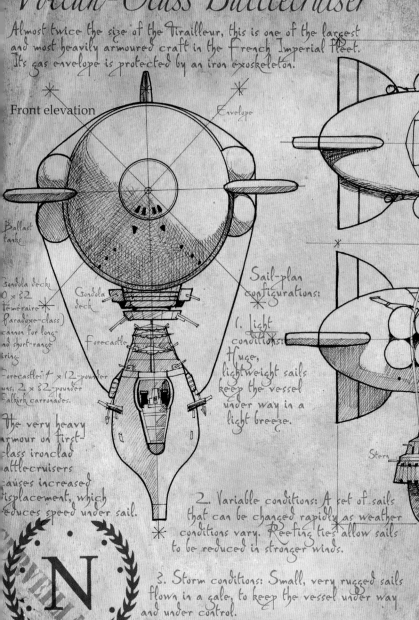

Front elevation

Envelope

Ballast tanks

Gondola deck:
10 × 22 *Téméraire* (*Paradoxe*-class) cannon for long- and short-range firing.

Forecastle: 4 × 12-pounder guns, 2 × 32-pounder Falkirk carronades.

Gondola deck

Forecastle

The very heavy armour on first-class ironclad battlecruisers causes increased displacement, which reduces speed under sail.

Stern

Sail-plan configurations:

1. Light conditions: Huge, lightweight sails keep the vessel under way in a light breeze.

2. Variable conditions: A set of sails that can be changed rapidly as weather conditions vary. Reefing ties allow sails to be reduced in stronger winds.

3. Storm conditions: Small, very rugged sails flown in a gale, to keep the vessel under way and under control.

THE ESCAPE PLAN

The first challenge for Arabella and Miles was how to get out of a permanently guarded room without being spotted. Arabella had noticed that the door guard didn't pay much attention to the faces of the slaves delivering supplies to the room, but only seemed concerned with counting them in and out. If they could capture a female who looked similar to her, Arabella could pretend to be her and slip out undetected. She recalled one girl, who'd delivered their lunch: tall, with brown eyes and chestnut hair worn long, just like Arabella's. The girl's nose had been a little too short and her lips a touch too thick, but there were ways to deal with that.

The problem was how to get Miles out. It was Ben who inadvertently suggested a solution. He was at work deep inside his generator, busy with some fiddly piece of machinery, when he suddenly cursed: 'Darn it! This toroidal transverse autotransformation coil for the energy accumulator is so darn fiddly I need the fingers of a child to do the windings!'

'Miles!' Arabella immediately cried. 'Could you pretend to be a child?'

'My lady, I really don't think…'

'Of course you could,' she coaxed, 'you're exactly the right size!'

Miles looked as disconcerted as his metal face would allow. 'I dare say there are music-hall automata who can carry off this type of masquerade for the entertainment of the masses,' he protested, 'but as a highly advanced Logical Englishman with a state-of-the-art analytical engine for a brain, I really consider such play-acting to be beneath my dignity.'

'You're a good sport, Miles,' said Arabella, and she went over and knocked on the door.

'We're hungry,' she said when the guard looked in. 'We could work a lot faster if we had some more of that stew. And can we have it delivered by that girl who served us lunch?'

'Why her?' the blunt-faced guard wanted to know.

Arabella hesitated. 'Er… because she has clean hands?'

The guard looked at her suspiciously.

'And we'll also need a child, about so high,' Arabella added, indicating a height approximating Miles's.

The guard continued to glare at her.

'Small hands,' she explained. 'Needed for the toroidal transformulator... er... coil thingie.'

Anything else?' grunted the guard.

'Yes, one more thing.' She handed him a cloth face mask. 'I suggest you put this on for the next few hours. We'll be mixing the gold with lots of nasty nitro-chloric acid, and the fumes, you know...' She wrinkled her nose. 'Not pleasant.'

The guard took the mask and shut the door.

Twenty minutes later the chestnut-haired girl arrived carrying a tray containing two bowls of watery stew. As soon as she set the tray down, Arabella seized her from behind, pinning her arms to her sides with one arm while clamping a hand to her mouth with the other. The woman wriggled and emitted muffled cries, which fortunately didn't reach the ears of the guard on the other side of the door. While Miles bound her with rope and placed some tape over her mouth, Arabella tried her best to reassure her.

'Please don't be alarmed, dear,' she said. 'We're not going to hurt you. I just need to pretend to be you for an hour or so. I'll be back before you know it, I promise.'

This did not soothe the girl as much as Arabella had hoped: she continued to struggle and make agitated noises, and her eyes widened in a worried, pleading sort of way.

In the midst of all this they heard footsteps approaching along the corridor outside, and Arabella hurriedly manhandled the girl behind one of the piles of junk. The girl was still squeaking hysterically, and Arabella had to press her hand tightly over her already-taped mouth to muffle the sound.

The door opened, and Arabella heard Miles exchange words with the guard. She peeped over the heap of scrap metal and saw a boy of about ten in prisoner blue standing in the open doorway, with the guard, now wearing his face mask, standing behind him. The guard was looking perplexed.

'Where is the prisoner who came in just now?' he demanded of Miles.

'Would that be... uh... the young lady who delivered the stew?' stalled Miles.

'Yeah. What happened to her?'

Miles clearly wasn't programmed to deal with this kind of subterfuge, and Arabella was unable to come over and help him, or else the kidnapped girl would start squeaking again. She waited desperately for Miles to say something – anything – but he seemed paralysed.

'What happened to her?' the guard repeated with growing impatience.

'What... happened to her indeed?' floundered Miles.

At that moment, with the guard looking ready to sound a full-scale 'escaped slave' alert, Ben suddenly popped his head up from the generator.

'She's in the lavatory,' he said, pointing to the door leading to the small room at the back of the workshop. 'I guess my logical friend here must be too English to feel able to make reference to such facts of life.'

The guard nodded. 'Here's the child you asked for,' he said, before departing the room and slamming the door.

At first the boy couldn't take his eyes off the Dread Eagle. Arabella watched as Ben eventually managed to coax him over to the generator, where he began to explain what he wanted the boy to do for him.

'Thanks for your help,' she called to Ben.

He looked up and winked at her. 'Hey, one good turn deserves another. You got me a kid with fingers just the right size!'

'I'm sorry, my lady,' said a dejected Miles, as he trundled over to where she and the girl were sitting. 'I fear I have disappointed you.'

'Not at all, Miles,' said Arabella, patting him affectionately on his cap. 'You are as your makers made you. I can't ask for more than that.'

She took her hand off her prisoner's mouth and the girl immediately began whimpering again. 'What do you think we should do with this girl?' she asked Miles. 'I don't think we can leave her here alone or she's bound to attract the attention of the guard.'

'Perhaps she wishes to communicate, my lady.'

When Miles said this, the girl began nodding her head vigorously.

Arabella removed the tape from her mouth, and the girl immediately launched into a long and breathless entreaty: 'Ma'am, I beg you not to hold me here. You must let me go this instant, for Mr Engelstad is expecting me at our usual trysting place in less than a quarter of an hour, and if I am not there, and with his jealous nature, he is sure to suspect the worst, though I have told him on many occasions that there is no other, which there certainly is not, but he will not believe me. If I do not show my face, as arranged, beneath the big clock on Stribog Terrace on Level Four at seven o'clock, he will convince himself that I am trysting with another. "Sally," he will say, "you have not been true." And nothing I can say or do will persuade him otherwise.'

Arabella bore all this with increasing irritation. When Sally had finished, she said tersely: 'Well, I'm very sorry, but you will have to rectify matters with Mr Engelstad later. I can assure you that my needs are of far greater moment.'

At this, Sally burst into very noisy tears. Arabella feared her sobs might alert the guards, so she grabbed the girl's shoulders and urgently assured her: 'I have no doubt that, given time, you will be able to demonstrate the constancy of your love to Mr Engelstad and the two of you will live happily ever after.'

Sally stopped crying and frowned. 'Love?' she said, as if shocked by the word. 'Happily ever after? You have misunderstood me, ma'am. I do not *love* Mr Engelstad. Far from it. But he *is* a senior guard and, being so, is a man of some influence here on Taranis. In exchange for a kiss from these lips once every evening at seven o'clock,' – she gave a shudder of revulsion as she said this – 'he has proved willing to do a great deal for myself and my fellow slaves in Jumala Wing, including extra rations, medicines and schoolbooks for the children. But if I don't appear at the designated time, he will denounce me as a Jezebel, and all of these benefits will instantly disappear.'

CHAPTER TWENTY-FOUR

THE
TRYST

Arabella stared at the girl as awareness dawned of what she would now have to do. Of course her plan to sabotage the Cloud Factory was more important than anything else – but what if she failed? Could she, in all conscience, risk denying the slaves of Jumala Wing their food and medicine, or their schoolbooks, for the sake of a plan that, according to Miles, had a vanishingly small chance of success? Of course she couldn't.

'The big clock,' she murmured to Sally, 'on Stribog Terrace…'

'On Level Four,' nodded the girl. She opened the silver cover of the timepiece that dangled from her necklace and anxiously glanced at it. 'I have to be there in ten minutes. Will you let me go?'

Arabella shook her head. 'I'll go,' she said. 'I'll pretend to be you.'

'How?' asked the startled Sally. 'We look nothing like each other.'

'I'll wear a face mask,' said Arabella. 'I'll pretend I've caught an infectious disease that I'm worried about passing on to him. That way he won't want to kiss me – thank goodness! – but at least he'll be assured of your fidelity.'

Sally shook her head fearfully. 'It is a terrible risk.'

'Better than not appearing at all. Now, where is this terrace?'

'Two floors down from here, then turn right along the corridor all the way to the end. Oh, are you sure about this, ma'am? Can anything be worth taking such a dreadful risk? If Mr Engelstad should find you out, he may kill us both or, worse, send us straight to Dr Bane.'

'He won't find out,' Arabella promised the girl, as she donned her face mask and removed the bowls of stew from the tray. She handed Miles his mask. It only partly covered his metal face, so she angled the peak of his cap downwards to throw the top part of his face into shadow. An inch-high metal exhaust tube still protruded from a hole in the top of his cap, but there was no time to do anything about that now.

'Can you try not to "smoke" too much while we're out there?' she asked him.

'I'll do my best, my lady,' said Miles, 'though I'm afraid movement does involve burning fuel, which in turn leads to smoke.'

'Hurry!' urged Sally. 'If you're going to do this, you must do it *now*!'

Suppressing any last-minute doubts, Arabella picked up the tray, marched over to the door, and knocked. The guard immediately opened the door. When he saw her, he stood aside to let her out. Now she would have to distract him, so he wouldn't look too closely at Miles.

'What are they doing in there, then?' she asked him, coarsening her vowels to disguise her upper-class accent.

'That's not for you to know,' said the guard.

'Oh, go on, give us a hint,' she said, fluttering her eyelashes. 'Why did they make me wear this mask?' As she said this, she felt Miles shuffle past behind her.

'Nitragoric acid or something,' muttered the guard. 'Now stop wasting my time. Go on, back to the kitchens with you... Who's that, then?' The guard was staring after Miles, who was already a fair distance along the corridor.

'That's the boy who came in earlier. They don't need him any more – I heard them say his fingers were too big.' Thanks to the dim lighting and the crookedness of the corridor, the guard seemed not to notice Miles's jerky, mechanical way of walking, and the faint plume of smoke emerging from the top of his cap.

Arabella quickly caught up with Miles, and they soon arrived at the top of a set of steep, spiral stairs. Miles was not very good with stairs, so, to save time, Arabella picked him up and began carrying him down the steps. He was heavy, and pain flared in her wound from the pressure of his weight on her arm. But, conscious that the clock was ticking perilously close to seven, she didn't dare stop.

Two flights down, they found themselves in another corridor. A speck of silvery outdoor light was visible at the far end. 'What's the time, Miles?' she asked him.

'A minute short of seven o'clock, my lady.'

'I'll have to run or I won't make it in time,' she told him. 'You come along to the terrace at your own pace and wait for me somewhere out of sight. Once I've managed to excuse myself from Mr Engelstad, we can make our way to the Cloud Factory. Agreed?'

'Agreed.'

Miles looked strangely vulnerable in his blue overall and cap, Arabella thought, and she couldn't resist giving his shoulder a friendly squeeze, even though she knew such a gesture could mean nothing to a logical gentleman like him. Then she turned and began running down the long corridor.

By the time she reached the open doors at the far end, she was utterly breathless. After taking a few seconds to compose herself, she stepped out onto a breezy Stribog Terrace. It was pleasant to see the sky again, even a creamy-smooth artificial sort of sky as presented by the interior of the cloud, and it instantly relaxed her. The terrace was similar to the one the Dread Eagle had originally brought her to – the same wooden floor interrupted by smokestacks – only this one was almost entirely empty of people. The only person present was a man, standing on the far side, beneath a giant clock. He was rocking on his heels, looking impatient. The clock stood at one minute past seven.

As she approached the man, he looked up and his face broke into a relieved smile. He was short in stature and, unlike most Taranite men, had a neat appearance, with carefully trimmed and combed hair and very white teeth. His grey guard's uniform, with its red epaulettes denoting his senior status, was spotless.

'You are late, my dear,' he called to her while she was still only halfway across the terrace. 'I was beginning to have my suspicions. And what are you wearing on your face?'

'A mask, Mr Engelstad,' she replied in a voice as similar to Sally's as she could manage. 'I have picked up a nasty bout of influenza. It's gone all around Jumala Wing. I feared I might pass it on to you.'

He looked puzzled. She stopped a few feet from him and was conscious of his eyes scrutinising every square inch of her visible face. Arabella was suddenly sure she would be found out.

'Why do you call me Mr Engelstad?' he asked her. 'What happened to *darling*? Or are you keeping that word for another man now, Sally?'

She shook her head vigorously. 'Of course not… darling. I – I – sometimes find it difficult to break the habit of formality.'

'Take off your mask,' he said, still frowning.

'I – what?'

'You heard me!' he thundered. 'Take off that mask. I want to see your face.'

'But I might make you sick.'

'Do you think I care about that?' he said. 'Do you have any idea how much these brief moments with you mean to me? What is a bout of flu next to a kiss from your lips?'

Arabella was thrown by this. She had yet to experience love for herself and found it hard to comprehend the power and madness of a thing that could cause someone to risk illness for the sake of a kiss.

'But, Mr Eng– I mean, darling! – I could not possibly allow you to take such a chance with your health.'

'Nonsense, my dear. Off with that mask, or do you want me to remove it for you?'

Mr Engelstad moved towards her and reached for the mask. She backed away, desperately trying to think of another excuse. 'Sir,' she blurted, 'I also have a boil next to my lip, a most unsightly carbuncle of such monstrous size that if you saw it, I fear you would never desire to look upon me again!'

'Show me your face!' he ordered, and, grabbing hold of the mask, he ripped it away.

He stared at Arabella's revealed features, seemingly stunned beyond the power of speech. She stared back, feeling like a thief exposed to the light, dreading his reaction, ready at any moment to flee back across the terrace and away down the corridor.

CHAPTER TWENTY-FIVE

THE SICKLY CHILD

For a moment they remained frozen like characters in a painting. Then the edges of Mr Engelstad's lips curled upwards and he began, rather disconcertingly, to smile. 'My dear,' he said, breathing deeply. 'You are not Sally, and this ought to upset me, but seeing your loveliness thus exposed, I am finding it hard right now to imagine how I could ever have fallen for such a girl. You are to her like a rose next to a common dandelion, or like a swan next to a goose. How can I go on hungering for mere bread after my eyes have tasted ambrosia? I do not know what brings you here, my angel – perhaps Sally had need of an alibi in order to go trysting with another – I no longer care. All that matters is that you are here, standing before me, the woman I have always longed for in my dreams, though never dared to imagine could exist.'

Listening to this, Arabella felt a deep blush rising within her. She had never been addressed in such a way, had never even thought of herself as pretty. She had always been a pilot first, a woman strictly second. Yet here she was, in unflattering overalls, caked in Taranite dust and dirt, and somehow the epicentre of this man's desires. But how could a person switch his affections so quickly? Was this how love worked? And if it did, how complicated this suddenly made things, and in all sorts of undesirable ways. Most seriously, it could spell disaster for Sally and her fellow inmates in Jumala Wing.

Mr Engelstad moved closer to her. He closed his eyes and rose up onto his tiptoes so that his lips were aligned with hers.

He's going to kiss me, thought Arabella in a sudden panic. She'd never been kissed by a man, and certainly didn't wish to start with Mr Engelstad.

'Mr Engelstad!' she cried, backing away from him just as he was moving in.

His eyes snapped open in surprise. 'Yes?' he said. 'What is it, my darling?'

'Mr Engelstad…' she said again, and she looked up at the sky, hoping for inspiration, but all she saw was the cloud.

And then, in a flash, it came to her. Whether she wanted it or not, she had power over this man. He could help her get into the Cloud Factory! But she had to be very careful about how she phrased her request.

'This is all my fault, Mr Engelstad,' she began. 'Please don't blame Sally. I persuaded her to let me take her place today. You see, she's told me about what a kind and generous man you are, and...'

'And?' he said, eyebrows raised expectantly.

'And I've always been passionate about clouds.'

'Clouds?' said Mr Engelstad, clearly bewildered by the strange turn the conversation had taken.

'Besotted with them – ever since I was a girl,' said Arabella, clasping her hands together in a fit of feigned enthusiasm. 'And ever since I was captured and brought here, I've often wondered about the cloud that surrounds Taranis – how it was made, how it always remains so perfect and still. So I was thinking, Mr Engelstad, since you've been so generous to Sally about food and medicines and suchlike – I was wondering if I could also beg a favour from you.'

She looked down briefly and bit her lip. Here came her big moment – this could land her, in one slick manoeuvre, right where she wanted, or right back in Dr Bane's torture chamber.

'I was wondering, Mr Engelstad, if you could allow me to see the room where you control the cloud.'

He looked at her incredulously. 'That's all you want? In return for a kiss?'

She nodded enthusiastically, then quickly added: 'As well as the usual things you do for Sally. Of course

I couldn't let my friend suffer for the sake of indulging this foolish fancy of mine.'

'I shall do as you ask,' said Mr Engelstad. 'I can't let you into the Cloud Factory itself – even *I* do not have that level of security clearance, it being one of the most secure locations in all Taranis – but I would be delighted to escort you to the viewing gallery, where you will be able to observe the cloud makers at work.'

'Oh, Mr Engelstad, you are so kind! How can I ever thank you!' Arabella's joy and relief came to a screeching halt as she noticed his lips were once again homing in on their desired target. With lightning reflexes, she intercepted his mouth with her forefinger, making him blink in surprise.

'Mr Engelstad,' she breathed in a pretence of pent-up passion. 'Would you mind if we waited until we were at the viewing gallery of the Cloud Factory? It would be so much more special for me if we could do this there.'

He smiled. 'Of course, my dear. We can go there now, if you like.'

They were stepping off the terrace and into the corridor when Mr Engelstad stopped in alarm. There, lurking in the shadows near the doors, he spotted the small figure of Miles.

'What have we here?' he exclaimed. 'Were you spying on us, boy?'

Miles emerged from his hiding place. 'I am sorry to have startled you, sir.'

Arabella put a protective arm around Miles's shoulders. 'He's my child, Mr Engelstad. I hope you don't mind that I brought him along.'

'Your ch–' choked Mr Engelstad. 'My dear, you look far too young.'

'You're too kind,' said Arabella, hurrying Miles along before Mr Engelstad got too close a look at him.

'Do I take it you are married, then?' asked Mr Engelstad, quickening his pace to keep up with her.

'Widowed,' replied Arabella quickly, disquieted by the amount of steam now rising from her child's cap. 'My husband was a sickly man. He had, er, excess water in his head, and in hot conditions this often turned to steam. I fear my son may have inherited the same affliction.'

Mr Engelstad gazed at Miles – the steam, the faint hissing sounds and the clunky way of walking. 'I'm very sorry for your child's… problems,' he said, as he showed them into an elevator reserved for the use of guards. It was a rickety old box with a squeaky door, and its gears grumbled alarmingly as they descended – but they survived the journey.

The second floor was rather crowded: the usual grey-uniformed guards and blue-overalled slaves were in evidence, as well as an unfamiliar breed of men who, from their white coats and generally distracted air, Arabella took to be scientists.

Mr Engelstad strode confidently along the corridors, with Arabella and Miles now trailing in his wake. The guards saluted as they passed him, the slaves lowered their heads, and the scientists ignored him.

'Nearly there now,' said Mr Engelstad, wetting his lips in anticipation of their expected reward. Arabella fretted over how she was going to shake the man off once he'd got them to their destination. Was she really going to have to kiss him? Oh, the things she had to do for her country!

Mr Engelstad led them through a set of swing doors to a quieter area, deserted except for a pair of guards standing in front of a locked steel door.

'Ah, here we are!' cried Mr Engelstad. 'The Cloud Factory!'

CHAPTER TWENTY-SIX

THE CLOUD FACTORY

Arabella walked over to a window, three feet high and about thirty feet long, to the right of the steel door. Through the window she saw a vast room containing eight enormous shining copper vats, each topped by steam-puffing chimneys with dome-shaped copper hats. Important-looking men with beards patrolled the room, inspecting clock displays with flickering needles attached to the sides of each vat, and recording the results on their clipboards. Other men fetched and carried trays laden with bottles of colourful liquids, while still others stood on step ladders and poured the contents of these bottles through hatchways at the top of each vat. A complex spaghetti of pipes led from each vat to the base of a fat golden pillar at the far end of the room.

The pillar had a diameter, at its base, of around five yards, and it rose into an enormous inverted cone with an ultimate diameter of at least twenty yards, where it disappeared into the roof.

'Observe,' said Mr Engelstad, 'the many and varied chemicals supplied in just the right proportions and at just the right temperatures by each of these copper vessels to the big cloud pump at the end there. I hope you are impressed, my dear.'

Arabella's gasp of awe was not entirely faked – the room certainly was impressive. It was also, she noted, highly vulnerable to sabotage. Cutting one of the feeder pipes to the pump, or changing the temperature settings on the vats, could seriously damage the cloud, if not destroy it.

'Are you ready to be kissed now, my love?' asked Mr Engelstad. His arms had grasped her shoulders, and he was pulling her towards his moist, slobbering lips. There was nothing she could do…

'Alphonse Engelstad!' screeched a female voice behind her. 'How dare you!'

Mr Engelstad froze. His lips dried and his face paled. He looked like a rat trapped in the path of an onrushing steam carriage.

Arabella turned to see a blonde-haired woman, dressed in prisoner blue, charging towards them through the swing doors. Her face was red with anger.

'Please excuse me, my dear,' mumbled Mr Engelstad, 'I've just realised I have to be somewhere else.' And with that he took off in the opposite direction, down a long, empty corridor.

'You worm!' the woman called after him. 'You philandering toad!' She stopped when she reached Arabella and glanced pityingly at her. 'Don't look so shocked, love!' she said. 'That's exactly what he is, and worse! I'll bet he compared you to a rose. I'll bet he said you were like ambrosia for his eyes. He said the same to me once – and half the slave women of Taranis. Trades their kisses for favours. Most of them are happy enough with extra food and stockings. But not me. My price for a kiss was marriage, and he promised it.' She gazed at his retreating figure. 'You promised me marriage, Alphonse!' she bellowed, and then she charged away after him.

'Help! Guards!' screamed Mr Engelstad as he saw her gaining on him. 'Arrest this madwoman!'

The two men guarding the steel door immediately left their post to dash off after her.

'Quick, Miles!' said Arabella. 'This is our chance! See if you can open the door.'

Miles trundled over to the steel door and inserted the skeleton key hidden inside his right index finger into the lock.

'My lady,' he said, as he worked. 'What will we do once we get in? The room is full of technicians. We will be spotted immediately.'

Arabella examined the room, tracing the route of the pipes with her eyes, when she noticed something.

'Some of the pipes from the vats run into the corners of the room,' she told Miles. 'I don't think they're visible to the people on the main floor. We could sneak around the edge and cut through those pipes, then escape – the damage won't be noticed until we've got away, and by then the cloud will hopefully be destroyed.' She turned excitedly to the automaton. 'This need not be a suicide mission, Miles. We might just live to tell the tale!'

'I wish I could share your confidence, my lady,' said Miles as his finger continued to work at the lock. 'I'm sorry to say my analysis of our predicament points to a far bleaker conclusion.'

'I'd be worried if it didn't,' she told him with a smile.

Miles shook his head. 'I never will understand how you humans can find amusement in danger,' he muttered. 'I warned you that we should never have embarked on this reckless venture. But, alas, it seems I am destined to play the role of Cassandra in your life: predicting each impending disaster, and doomed always to be mocked or ignored.'

Arabella was thinking about this remark and watching Miles at work, when she gradually became aware of a gentle hissing sound behind her. It stopped and started, almost like breathing. It reminded her of something.

And then she remembered…

Someone was standing right behind them, watching them – someone calm, focused and infinitely patient –

a thin man with a stovepipe hat, dark goggles and a leather mask.

Turning, she caught sight of his henchman first – the giant with the bald head and no neck. He reached out to her with his big arms and enveloped her in a crushing hold. Thus imprisoned, she was turned to face Commodus Bane. The torturer fixed her with his inky-black insect eyes, his steel fist hissing as it opened and closed.

'Ah! Lady Arabella West,' he chuckled. 'The traitor's daughter. What a pleasant surprise! Thought you'd make a little mischief with our cloud, did you? Mr Forrester not keeping you busy enough, hmm? No, well it turns out Mr Forrester never had any need for you anyway. He's told me everything, and I didn't even have to torture him. More's the pity! An attack of sentiment, he called it. Didn't want to see that aristocratic skin of yours go to waste.'

Bane reached out with his human hand and stroked her cheek admiringly.

'Well, I can think of some uses for it,' he murmured. 'A new cover for my lampshade, for instance. But without Mr Forrester as your protector, you would seem to be rather short of friends around here, young lady. You're what the Sky Magister would call a "useless eater". You eat, but you have no use. Normally, we kill useless eaters, but I believe you have some information for us concerning the *Nelson*, and I shall enjoy extracting that from you now. As for your tin friend, he's heading straight for the scrapyard.'

Without further warning, Bane darted over to where Miles was standing by the door. He raised his steel arm high in the air and brought it down hard on Miles's head. Miles crashed to the floor, a severe dent in his cranium. Bane crouched by the stricken automaton and hammered his arm down several more times, smashing at the joints of Miles's arms and legs until he was little more than a mess of metal body parts, sprouting wires, pipes and springs. Pinioned as she was by the giant, Arabella could only stare in horror at what had been done to her logical friend.

CHAPTER TWENTY-SEVEN

THE PAIN INSIDE

Arabella lay slumped on the stone floor of her cell, more wretched than she'd felt since the death of her father. She was in terrible pain from burns to her arms and legs. Her tongue was so dry it had become stuck to the roof of her mouth. But these discomforts were as nothing compared to the pain inside. She had betrayed her country. She had given away national secrets. Her image of herself as a brave heroine, willing to martyr herself for Britain, had proved an illusion. At some point during the long hours of her torture, it had all become too much – she had started talking. She had told Bane what he wanted to know – that she was a spy, that there was a concerted British effort to find and destroy the Dread Eagle, that HMAS *Nelson* would be taking off tomorrow at dawn from Weymouth, heading for Granville. She hadn't said any more, but only because the pain had become so bad she could no longer speak.

In a matter of hours, thanks to her, the flagship of the Royal Air Fleet would sail blithely into the sky towards its doom. The only consolation was that she probably wouldn't be around to see it – she assumed they would execute her before it happened. Oh yes, she didn't need Miles around to tell her that things were looking bleak. Poor Miles – he might have been made of metal and wires, but he'd been her friend, and she was pained by the casual way that Bane had destroyed him.

From further along the corridor came a full-throated scream – Commodus Bane was back at work, his hot, glowing finger extracting secrets. She had no doubt there were all sorts of secrets to be extracted in a place like this – information about cargo-vessel routes; slave rebellions being planned; plots being hatched to amputate Bane's metal arm and force him to eat it...

She tried to move her tongue to swallow, but couldn't. If she didn't have something to drink soon, she would surely die. The cell, like her mood, was dark and dismal – lit by a small, grimy gas lamp that hung from the ceiling and left everything in shadow except a small circle of floor in the centre of the room. From the dim corners she could hear the tiny scufflings of mice, and from neighbouring cells came the groans, mumbles and snores of her fellow prisoners. She added to the chorus with an involuntary moan of her own. What she would give for some cream to soothe the burning!

Then a different kind of sound reached her ears – footsteps approaching along the corridor. They stopped outside her cell. It was too dark to see who was out there, but she guessed it was her executioner. She braced herself, determined at least to face her final moments bravely. Then she heard a florid male voice murmur: 'My darling, you stand above the other women on Taranis like a rose in a field of dandelions, like a swan in a herd of geese.'

Mr Engelstad! What in heaven was he doing down here? If he was trying to persist with his courtship of her, his timing was poor! But perhaps he could bring her a drink of water. Right now, that would be worth a dozen kisses!

'Monsieur, you are too kind,' came a woman's voice – and Arabella realised that he'd found a new object for his insatiable lips. The French-accented female voice also sounded familiar to her.

'Can I kiss you now?' pleaded Mr Engelstad.

'You may.'

Arabella shuddered at the prolonged, wet slurping sound that followed.

'Thank you, my dear!' Mr Engelstad breathed eventually.

'Now will you let me in?' the woman asked.

'Of course.'

A key rattled in the lock and the door squeaked open, then clanged shut. The woman's appearance gradually revealed itself as she stepped into the glow cast by the gas lamp. Arabella's heart gave a little surge when she saw who it was. Marie Daguerre was carrying a pitcher of water in one hand and dragging a heavy sack with the other. After depositing these items on the floor, she came over and embraced Arabella, kissing her on both cheeks.

Arabella found she was too weak to get up. She made a feeble gesture towards the pitcher, and Marie immediately brought it over to her. The girl held it up to her lips and the first drops passing onto her tongue were like pure, sweet rain straight from heaven.

'Thank you,' Arabella croaked.

Marie seated herself beside Arabella. From her pocket she took out a jar of calamine lotion and began gently applying the cooling cream to Arabella's arms and legs. Arabella closed her eyes and savoured the soothing sensation on her skin. But as the physical pain began to ease, her emotional torment intensified and she began to cry.

'I'm so sorry, am I hurting you?' asked Marie.

'No, no. It feels good. But no lotion can relieve the pain I feel inside. I – I have betrayed my country, Marie,' sobbed Arabella.

'There is no shame in that,' said Marie. 'Every person in this hellish place has betrayed someone or something. That monster Bane makes cowards and traitors of us all. That is his aim – to prove that courage and nobility do not exist.'

'He has certainly proved that in my case,' snivelled Arabella.

'Nonsense,' said Marie. 'You are the bravest girl I know. Many strong men have cracked within one hour in that room. You were in there for more than two. And you have more wounds than I have ever seen on a body.'

She took some more cream from the jar and resumed her tender massage. 'You were also very brave to try to break into the Cloud Factory earlier,' Marie added. 'I am sorry, I should never have encouraged you in such a foolish endeavour.'

'I'm very glad you did,' replied Arabella. 'For a while back there, I really felt as though I was doing something useful.' She peered up at the soft-eyed, terribly thin girl and felt a sudden rush of concern for her. 'You should go now,' Arabella told her. 'You'll be in trouble if they catch you here.'

'I am safe for three hours,' said Marie. She could not suppress a nervous giggle. 'My kiss bought me that much. Monsieur Engelstad has influence over the guards down here. They will turn a blind eye.'

'He certainly has proved useful,' agreed Arabella. 'But I'm sorry you had to kiss him.'

'Well, at least it wasn't as bad as a session with Dr Bane,' said Marie. 'Not *quite* as bad, anyway.'

'What's in the sack?' Arabella asked her.

Marie reached over and pulled it open so Arabella could see inside.

'Miles!' she said, spotting the top of his head.

'Pieces of Miles,' Marie corrected her. 'I am friends with the slaves who were ordered to send him down to the incinerator. I persuaded them to pack him up and give him to me instead.'

'Thank you!' said Arabella. She gave her a hug, then winced at the pain this caused her. 'But I'm afraid I wouldn't know how to put him back together.'

'Then it's lucky you know me, isn't it?' said Marie. She stood up and took a theatrical bow. 'May I introduce myself: Marie Daguerre, *Ingénieur en Mécanique, Première Classe*! In my previous life I was a specialist in making and repairing anything, from steam carriages to aethercell devices. I'm sure automata cannot be so very different.'

Arabella smiled and thought how lucky she was to have encountered this girl – spy, nurse, mender of broken spirits, and now, it turned out, engineer – perhaps things weren't as bad as they seemed.

Marie wiped the cream off her hands onto her trousers and went to work on Miles. Arabella watched as the girl opened up his chest cavity and peered deep into the intricate, labyrinthine world of automaton anatomy. Marie seemed unfazed by the millions of tiny gears, levers, wires and springs, the brass rods, screws, tubes, pins, rivets and bolts that all combined to form the remarkable entity known as Miles.

With the aid of her pocket tool kit, Marie went to work reconnecting, reattaching, mending, testing, adjusting, retesting and fine-tuning. More than once, she stopped and scratched her head, muttering: 'British engineering... very eccentric!' At one point, Miles's voice eerily emerged from his detached head: 'Mary had a little lamb, Its fleece as white as... My lady, I am feeling a little unwell.'

In the course of her work, Marie made a series of extraordinary discoveries relating to Miles's left hand. She demonstrated to Arabella how the hand could automatically detach itself from his arm and then move about under its own steam on a set of tiny rollers embedded in the palm, powered by a little engine in the base of the thumb. Furthermore, concealed in the tip of the middle finger she found a miniature dry-plate camera, and in the tip of the index finger was a microphone that could actually record sounds on a little wax cylinder buried in one of the knuckles.

'I had no idea!' gasped Arabella as all this was revealed.

'Some of these things I have never seen before,' murmured Marie, 'not even in theoretical papers.'

'That's British engineering,' smiled Arabella – 'eccentric, and ingenious!'

Amazingly, the sounds of all Marie's industry did not attract the attention of any guards – Mr Engelstad had been true to his word. But, as the three hours of Marie's visit drew to an end, she was forced to speed up her work, and only just managed to complete it, connecting the last seal on Miles's hip joint as the guard arrived to open the cell door.

Arabella's spirits slumped as she heard the key in the lock and the creak of the door opening.

'I hope I have done a fair job on your friend,' said Marie, climbing to her feet.

'I'm sure you have,' said Arabella, mustering a small smile. 'Thank you! I don't know what good it will do me, or Miles, but at least I have him back with me.'

The girl handed her the jar of calamine lotion. 'Use this on your wounds when they feel sore.'

Arabella thanked her again. 'You have been a good friend, Marie. Good luck with your life. I wish I could have done more for you.'

'Come on! Outta there!' called the guard.

Marie had tears in her eyes as she embraced Arabella. 'Be brave, *ma chérie*,' she sniffed. 'I pray to God there may yet be some way out of this – for you, for all of us.'

PART IV

18 JULY 1845

CHAPTER TWENTY-EIGHT

THE
HAND

Nervously, Arabella pressed the switch on Miles's back. The engine began to gurgle, and the electric yellow life-light flickered, then shimmered from his eyes. The light seemed a little darker and less steady than before.

'How are you feeling, little man?' she asked.

'Greetings, my lady,' he said after a short pause. His voice was lower, and slower. 'I feel… tampered with. Has someone been tinkering with my insides?'

'You were smashed up by Commodus Bane,' explained Arabella.

'Yes, I remember,' said Miles, his voice sinking even lower.

'My friend kindly put you back together.'

Miles vibrated uncomfortably.

'Was your friend... French, by any chance?'

'Yes! It was Marie Daguerre, the girl who gave us that map to the Cloud Factory. How did you know?'

'There are... French ways of doing things,' Miles said in slightly strangled tones.

'Oh! I do hope that it won't change you too much. I did rather like the way you were, Miles. And you are, after all, a Logical *Englishman*!'

'Have no fear, my lady. I remain both logical and English to my core. Her meddling, thankfully, did not extend as far as my brain. As for the rest of me...' He tried flexing his joints, and it may have been Arabella's imagination, but she thought she detected a disturbingly Gallic shrug of his shoulders. Miles, however, pronounced himself satisfied.

'I'm very relieved to hear it,' said Arabella, 'though I'm afraid it may all be to little avail.' She told him of her betrayal of the *Nelson*'s course, and her impending execution. 'Even I can find little positive to say about our current prospects,' she admitted.

'That in itself is a positive sign, my lady. For you are now, at last, seeing things as they really are. This bodes well for the future.'

'What future?' sighed Arabella.

'Whatever future remains to us – which does, admittedly, appear to be a brief one. It is now 12.30 a.m. The *Nelson* will depart at dawn, in four and a half hours' time. I estimate the attack will take place some thirty minutes after that. Until then, and for some hours afterwards, I calculate that the Taranite leaders will be focusing all their attention on the capture of the *Nelson* and its aftermath. I therefore very much doubt that you will be executed before 9 o'clock in the morning. That gives us eight and a half hours to try to save ourselves.'

'What can we possibly do stuck in here?'

'The first thing that you can do, my lady, is to get some sleep.'

She stared at him. 'Are you sure Marie didn't do something to your brain, Miles? What good will sleeping do? And how can I possibly sleep, knowing I'm going to die in the morning?'

'You will need your energy for what may come later, my lady,' said Miles. 'For the next few hours there is nothing you can do, so the most logical course of action is to sleep.'

Arabella stamped her foot. 'If you have a plan, my metal friend, would you do me the kindness of sharing it with me?'

Miles stared placidly back at her. 'I have no plan, my lady. But I do have a few… accessories… that I may be able to deploy to our advantage. Information-gathering, so to speak.'

'And what accessories might they be?'

Miles said nothing.

'Come along now, Miles! Don't be coy! Might this, by any chance, have anything to do with that clever hand of yours?'

'If you are referring to my lock-picking finger, I do not believe that this is applicable to our current circumstances – not with a guard standing right outside our cell.'

'I'm talking about your *left* hand, Miles.'

The automaton seemed to shudder slightly.

'I know about the camera and the microphone and the recording device,' she murmured.

'That is top-secret technology, my lady,' said Miles quietly. 'Does the French girl know about it?'

'Yes. But she's trustworthy.'

'Trustworthy or not, this is a most unfortunate development. My superiors will not be pleased.' Miles made a soft beeping sound that she interpreted as a sigh. 'We must try to ensure that knowledge of this spreads no further.'

He pressed a concealed button on his left wrist and the brass hand slipped off. 'I would like to gather any information I can about the progress of the Aetheric Shield and the Sky Magister's plans for the *Nelson*'s capture.' He placed the hand on the floor and pressed some buttons on a barely visible keyboard recessed within the palm – feeding instructions, Arabella assumed, into the hand's navigational brain.

Carrying it over to the cell door, Miles passed the hand through the feeding hatch near the bottom of the door and let it drop to the floor of the corridor outside. Arabella watched as its tiny, almost silent engine coughed into life and, with a little puff of steam, the hand began moving on its rollers towards the dungeon exit.

'This will take a few hours,' said Miles. 'In the meantime, I suggest again that you try to get some sleep.'

Arabella nodded and seated herself on the floor. Now that her thirst was quenched and the pain from the burns had subsided, her predominant physical need did appear to be sleep – in truth, she was exhausted.

'Well,' she yawned, as she settled herself down, 'wake me up as soon as you have any news.'

'I will, my lady.'

Arabella was awakened by a strange, jittery light playing over her eyelids. She opened them and saw, like a moving painting above her head, the ghostly form of Ben Forrester, staring back at her with his intense, dark eyes. Was this a dream? Was she *dreaming* about the young man now? How perfectly ridiculous! Of all the people to dream about on the last night of her life!

That second thought hit her like a cold thud to the chest.

Was she dead already, then? Was this the afterlife? No, it couldn't be. It was beyond the realms of possibility that she and Mr Forrester could share the same afterlife. She imagined heaven as a place of beautifully mown English lawns and white-painted garden furniture and immaculate butlers serving cream teas. Or else she imagined it as an endless summer sky with wispy little clouds, through which she would fly in her *Comanche Prince* above a patchwork of English farms and villages.

There would never be a place in her heaven for Mr Forrester!

'My lady!'

Ah, Miles! Yes, there might be a place for him. He could play the butler.

'My lady! Wake up and take a look at this.'

Arabella blinked and sat up. The dream hadn't faded. There was Mr Forrester, still moving about, as if by magic, on the wall of her cell. He seemed to be made of light, a yellowish, sepia sort of light that flickered as it shone. Could Miles see this as well? She turned to him and was shocked to discover that the light was emanating from a cavity in his stomach area. A lamp was sitting there, inside his abdomen, flashing and whirring busily.

CHAPTER TWENTY-NINE

THE MAGIC PICTURE SHOW

'It's like a zoetrope,' Miles explained. 'If you run a series of still images one after another, it can give the impression of movement. The pictures have been developed on a transparent medium called celluloid, and passed in front of a gas lamp fitted with a shutter and a lens.'

'But – but where did you get these pictures of Mr Forrester?'

'My hand brought them back a short while ago,' answered Miles. 'They were recorded in the throne room of Odin's palace. Now, if we synchronise the images with the sound recording the hand made at the same time, we can hear what Mr Forrester is saying.'

Miles pressed some more buttons on his left hand, now reattached to his wrist, and twirled a few knobs in his stomach cavity. There came a quiet crackle and hiss, and suddenly Mr Forrester was speaking.

'As I will now demonstrate, Mr Sky Magister, sir,' spoke the jittery sepia image of Ben, 'the Dread Eagle is now fully protected by the Aetheric Shield. Your men may fire at it whenever they wish.'

For the first time, Arabella noticed, towering above Ben in the background of the picture show, the awesome figure of *Horus*, the Dread Eagle. To the left of the raptor she could see the completed Aetheric Shield Generator, with the cauldron above it, suspended from a horizontal pole supported by the two wooden scaffolding towers. A rope fixed to the lip of the cauldron had been pulled down, tipping the cauldron forward, and a thin stream of liquid was pouring from it into a fuzzy, confusing shape hovering between the five electromagnetic towers – the Aethersphere portal. Even seen through the medium of this magical zoetrope, the Aethersphere's shape made no sense, seeming to resemble many things and nothing at the same time.

Emerging on the right of the screen were a dozen armed guards, looking puny next to the Dread Eagle. They took aim at the bird with their volley guns and, at the given order, began to fire. As before, the bullets hit an invisible wall a foot from the bird's steel feathers, and began to drift very slowly, as if through oil or some other dense medium. The soldiers tried blasting the eagle with flame guns, and the fire, as it neared the target, became motionless, as if time itself had warped around the bird.

Despite herself, Arabella found herself sucked into the drama of these events unfolding on her cell wall. It was quite extraordinary that transparent daguerreotypes, projected one by one by a lamp onto an ordinary wall, could create a gripping spectacle, as enthralling as any stage play.

Next up came the heavy artillery. Four breech-loading Armstrong cannon were wheeled to within point-blank range. These fearsome weapons, Arabella knew, could pierce the exoskeleton of a *Volcan*-class battlecruiser. Yet, when the smoke cleared, the Dread Eagle's feathers remained pristine.

After the tests were complete, the Sky Magister himself approached Ben, a fierce grin on his face. He clasped Ben's hand in his. Ben smiled back, and it made Arabella feel sick to see the pair standing there in front of the Dread Eagle, like evil brothers.

Odin looked as if he were about to say something, but they didn't get a chance to hear him. Several pairs of footsteps were approaching along the corridor outside. Miles swiftly doused his magic lamp and cut its engine. The moving pictures and the sounds faded as if they had never been, leaving nothing but an ordinary wall of painted brick.

A key rattled in the lock, their cell door opened and a new prisoner was pushed inside. He fell to the floor, rolled over once, then looked up and smiled.

'Hey! If it isn't Lady Arabella – and Miles! What do you know! The old gang's back together!'

Ben Forrester didn't look too upset, considering his new circumstances.

The door banged shut again and the key turned with a heavy click.

'Mr Forrester!' said Arabella when she found her voice again. 'This is a surprise! I thought you were thick as thieves with the Sky Magister.'

Ben laughed as he climbed to his feet and dusted himself down. 'Oh, he liked my shield all right. But once it was his, he no longer had any need of me. I'll probably be executed, or maybe I'll end up as a slave in the engine room, which from what I've heard amounts to more or less the same thing. You were right, ma'am: that contract wasn't worth the paper it was written on.'

'That part of it does not surprise me,' said Arabella. 'What I find astonishing is that you ever believed it was worth more than that. Could you not see the ludicrous vulnerability of your position: trapped on a floating city with a bunch of cut-throat pirates with nothing but a piece of paper to serve as protection? Still, I suppose this is where your worship of money leads you.'

Ben nodded thoughtfully, though he displayed none of the sorrow or remorse she had hoped and expected to see. Arabella felt compelled to go on, if only to make him understand the full extent of what he had done.

'So,' she said, 'the *Nelson* will shortly be captured, and then there will be nothing to stop the French from invading. You can go to your grave, sir, knowing that you, personally, are responsible for the defeat and enslavement of an entire nation.'

As she was saying this, it struck her that exactly the same thing could be said of her. Suddenly feeling pale and weak, Arabella leaned back against the wall. 'And I am just as guilty, if not more so,' she said with trembling lips. 'If you provided Odin with a vital weapon for his attack, I have furnished him with the time and the place.'

Ben looked up, surprised. 'You, ma'am?'

She nodded. 'My crime is far worse than yours, Mr Forrester. You never had a country to betray, as I did.'

Then she saw him staring at the angry red welts on her arms. She quickly covered them up.

'You were tortured – again!' he groaned. 'Oh, ma'am!'

'Never mind about that!' said Arabella, who hated the thought of anyone feeling sorry for her. 'What I must do now – and you can help me if you wish – is to try and put right what I have done. What is the time, Miles?'

'4.55 a.m., my lady.'

Arabella gasped. 'Then the *Nelson* will depart in just five minutes, and the attack will take place in the next half-hour! We have no time to lose. Miles, can you get us out of here?'

'I could open the cell door,' answered the automaton, 'but as there are guards out there, it would avail us nothing.'

'I can distract them,' suggested Ben.

'Good idea!' said Arabella, pleased that he was coming on board.

'It would have to be a very big distraction, sir,' said Miles, 'as there are three guards on duty, and another door to get through at the far end of the corridor. It will take me two minutes to break through each door.'

Ben thought for a moment. 'If Lady Arabella and I stage a fight, that'll lure one of the guards in here. Soon as he opens the door, I'll overpower him while you two make a run for the second door, and...'

'And what about the other two guards?' asked Miles.

Ben frowned, and lapsed back into thought.

'I'll divert them by running in the other direction,' said Arabella suddenly.

'But, my lady, that will take you towards...'

'Towards Commodus Bane, I know! It will be the last thing they'll expect. While they're chasing me down, you, Miles, will break open the lock. Wait for me outside the dungeon door – I'll try and give them the slip, then meet you there.'

An anxious puff of steam rose from Miles's hat. 'Very well, my lady. If you really think that is the only way...'

CHAPTER THIRTY

THE
FIGHT

'If you'll allow *me*, ma'am,' said Ben, 'I'd like to throw my hat in the ring and join your little escape party.'

'You'll be very welcome, Mr Forrester,' said Arabella, pleased. 'Now, if that's all the planning done, I suppose we'd better start our fight.'

'Indeed we had,' Ben nodded, with a mischievous smile. 'After you, your ladyship.'

Of all the people she might have reasons to fight with, Ben Forrester had to be high on the list, and yet she was, at first, stumped for words.

But then something floated into her head – some words Commodus Bane had said to her: ... *it turns out Mr Forrester never had any need for you anyway. He's told me everything, and I didn't even have to torture him... An attack of sentiment, he called it. Didn't want to see that aristocratic skin of yours go to waste.*

Suddenly, she didn't just want to stage a fight with him – she wanted to murder him!

'You gave me up to Bane without a fight!' she hissed. 'You cut me loose to save your own skin! You *knew* I was going to be tortured, and you didn't care!'

'Wait! Wait!' said Ben, holding up his hands in a calming gesture. 'Is this for real now, lady? Or are you just play-acting?'

'You know it's for real,' Arabella said in a quietly menacing voice. 'You're a snake. I don't know how you can live with yourself.'

Ben was staring at her, looking genuinely perplexed. He scratched his head. 'I may be many things you don't exactly approve of, ma'am, but I am not a snake, and I did not give you up to Bane! I've never even met the man, let alone spoken to him. If he told you that I gave you up to him, then – then he's a goddam liar!'

'You *would* say that, wouldn't you?' she screamed. 'But why should I believe you, Mr Forrester, when you yourself don't believe in anything? Hmm? Give me one good reason!'

An irritated-looking guard strode up to the cell door. 'Hey, pipe down in there, will you?' he barked.

Quick as a cat, Ben sprang at Arabella, seizing her by her collar and pushing her roughly against the door of the cell. The force of the push knocked the breath from her lungs. His mouth, inches from hers, was twisted into a scowl, upper lip twitching with barely contained fury. 'Get this she-devil out of here!' he bellowed. 'She's a witch, I'm telling you! Get her out!'

His anger frightened and impressed her at the same time. It made her shiver inside, being this close to him and seeing all that violent hatred in his face. That couldn't all be acting, could it?

Whatever it was, it did the trick. The guard opened the door, and a second later Ben leapt on him and pinned him to the ground.

'Go!' Ben screamed at Arabella and Miles. They dashed out into the corridor. Miles turned left, towards the dungeon exit, while Arabella spun right. All along the corridor the other prisoners started shouting and beating on the doors of their cells, adding to the chaos. The other two guards, who had been playing cards at a little table, began climbing to their feet as Arabella ran full pelt towards them. The sight of her charging deeper into the dungeon must have shocked them. They grabbed at her, but too late – they could do nothing to stop her forward momentum. She barged past them, knocking over their table and sending the cards flying. This brought a huge cheer from the watching prisoners.

Before she knew it, Arabella was pushing open the big oak door at the end of the corridor and falling through it into Bane's torture chamber. The room was dark and silent, the fire now just embers. Bane was nowhere to be seen, thank goodness. He must have gone up to join the Sky Magister as he prepared to celebrate the capture of the *Nelson*. Yet just the sight of the room and the table, and the lingering smell of burnt flesh, were enough to make her skin prickle into goosebumps. Hearing a movement behind her, Arabella quickly dived into the shadows on one side of the room. It was so dark here, she could barely make out her surroundings. One of the men entered, holding a gas-powered torch – she guessed his colleague must have gone after either Miles or Ben. The guard swung the torch around the room and its beam flashed inches above her head.

'I know you're here, missy!' he called. 'Just give yourself up, why don't you, and I'll be gentle with you this time, I promise.' She caught a glimpse of a wolfish, yellow-toothed grin.

After kicking over a few chairs and peering under tables, he became more methodical, moving carefully around the edge of the room, gradually approaching her hiding place. She edged leftwards, trying always to keep beyond the range of his torch. After reaching the corner, she began creeping along the wall containing the fireplace. Her plan was to keep moving around the room until she reached the entrance again, then make a dash for the dungeon door, which hopefully Miles would have opened by this time.

But then, a few yards along the wall, her hands encountered a curtain, and beyond it a recess of some kind. She could feel a small wooden step in the recess, and above it another – a private staircase for Commodus Bane.

And an escape route for her!

But what about Miles and Ben?

The guard was getting closer again, so she quickly pushed through the curtain and seated herself on the first and second steps. The staircase spiralled upwards above her into complete darkness. She risked a peek from behind the curtain – and got quite a fright...

A small, dark shape, about the size of a rat, was speeding across the floor, making directly for her. The guard saw it too, and fired his pistol at it. The bullet ricocheted off the stone floor and buried itself in a wall somewhere beyond.

The guard cursed. 'Flamin' rats!'

The shape hit the curtain just below her foot, making her jerk back in revulsion. But then she noticed its dull brassy gleam and, with a rush of excitement, recognised it as Miles's hand.

Stealthily, she pushed her own hand through the bottom of the curtain and pulled the metal hand through. It felt warm, and she could feel the quiet throb of its engine in the base of the thumb. At her touch, a little light came on in the tip of the middle finger, and a faint crackle could be heard. The hand was recording.

She held it so that the fingertip camera was pointing at her face, and whispered: 'I'm in Bane's room. There's a guard...'

Suddenly, the curtain was ripped back, and her eyes were seared by the full glare of the guard's torch.

CHAPTER THIRTY-ONE

THE HUMILIATING SPECTACLE

'**G**otcha!' yelled the guard, grinning like a hyena. He raised his pistol and reached towards Arabella. Without thinking, she raised Miles's hand and brought it down hard on the guard's head. The guard continued to grin for a few more seconds, before keeling over unconscious.

She brought the fingertip camera back in front of her face, surprised at how calm she felt, and said: 'Don't worry about the guard... I've found a private staircase in Bane's room that can get us out of here and hopefully straight up to Odin's palace. Meet me here as soon as you can.'

She placed the hand, palm downwards, back on the floor, and it raced across the room and out of the door.

A minute later, Ben came running into the room, followed by Miles. Arabella swished back the curtain and beckoned to them.

'What about the other guards?' she asked.

'We've dealt with them,' said Ben.

'Mr Forrester rendered them both unconscious,' said Miles.

Arabella looked up at Ben, surprised and impressed. 'Not bad – for a salesman,' she remarked.

Ben shrugged modestly. 'I did a little jujitsu when I was younger.' Then he gestured at the prostrate figure of the guard. 'And not bad yourself – for an air artiste.'

She didn't meet his eyes, still feeling tense with him after their fight. Her feelings about Ben Forrester were very confused – he seemed to be so many things. A big part of her wanted to hate and distrust this smiling, profit-driven salesman, who could well have given her up to Bane to save his own skin. But that image of him didn't quite tally with the charmingly reckless spirit who flew into Taranis two days ago in his battered air carriage, mocking the Sky Magister even as he peddled him his wares. And she thought she'd glimpsed a deeper side to him, too, beneath the carefree exterior – his anger with himself for not attempting to rescue her from Bane, for example, and the tightlipped fury that had possessed him just now after she'd accused him of betraying her. Mr Forrester was certainly an enigma, and one that irritated, charmed, unnerved and intrigued her all at the same time.

'My lady, it is now 5.20 a.m.,' said Miles. 'The attack on the *Nelson* may already have happened.'

'Then we had better get moving,' said Arabella.

Miles eyed the steep spiral staircase and puffed morosely. 'I will slow you both down,' he said.

'Nonsense, little fella!' said Ben. 'I'll carry you.' And he hoisted the Logical Englishman onto his back.

Arabella led the way. It was a long, tiring climb up the tight, twisting wooden staircase. They finally emerged, not in Odin's palace, but on a deserted terrace. A quick glance around her told Arabella that they were roughly two-thirds of the way up the giant mound of tiered terraces that lay between the base of the city and its apex, where Odin's palace was situated. The uppermost terraces, closest to the palace, were thronged with Taranites. At the very top, she could just make out the tall, muscular figure of Odin and, by his side, the thin Commodus Bane in his black cloak and stovepipe hat. They, and everyone else, were looking out towards the wall of the cloud that surrounded Taranis.

Arabella followed their gaze, in time to witness the most spectacular and soul-destroying sight of her entire young life.

The giant Dread Eagle, *Horus*, was at that moment emerging from the cloud wall, accompanied by an escort of twenty smaller Dread Eagles that fanned out to either side of him. Each eagle had a warcraft of the Royal Air Fleet gripped in its talons. Clasped in the claws of *Horus* was the iron exoskeleton of HMAS *Nelson*, the air fleet's flagship.

Arabella had seen paintings of the *Nelson*, but nothing could have prepared her for its overwhelming power and majesty. The giant battlecruiser's exoskeleton, housing the gas envelope, had a sharp, 50-foot spike for a prow, sweeping fins along its sides, gun turrets fore and aft and two rows of steam-cannon portholes running the length of its vast flanks. The gondola beneath was a 500-foot copper-coloured battleship of the air, with tiers of platforms and turrets rising above its gleaming hull. The entire vessel bristled with powerful, state-of-the-art weaponry, yet it had been rendered impotent against the aetherically shielded Dread Eagle.

Witnessing the pride of Britain humbled like this, to be laid at the feet of the savage pirate king Odin like a common war trophy, was, for Arabella, utterly humiliating. Like seeing a lion in the jaws of a jackal, it seemed a complete inversion of the natural order. The salt in the wound was the knowledge that she had been partly responsible for the catastrophe.

Shaking, and with tears in her eyes, she turned to Ben. 'We're too late,' she whispered.

Arabella was surprised – and disturbed – at how calm he appeared. But then she reminded herself that his only aim had been to escape from the dungeon. What did he care about the fate of all these vessels and their crews?

She looked up in awe and dismay as the shadow of the vanquished flagship fell across Taranis. *Horus* was leading the flock of Dread Eagles and their captive craft towards a large public space at the very apex of the city, right in front of Odin's palace. The eagles ascended towards this summit in perfect formation. She could see ropes dangling from holes in the bellies of the birds, down which Taranite pirates must have descended in order to board the warcraft of the air fleet. Just visible from where Arabella was standing were the crews of the captured vessels, lined up on the gondola decks with the guns of the pirate boarding parties trained upon them.

From the Sky Magister's point of view, it had been a flawlessly executed operation. With this dramatic coup, he had announced himself as a man of international consequence, to be feared by even the strongest military powers. Arabella dreaded to imagine what ransom Odin would demand from the British for the return of all these vessels and their crews.

The Dread Eagles, with great pumps of their enormous wings, finally reached the summit of Taranis, and all twenty-one of them, with *Horus* in the middle, hovered above the palace square, ready to descend. The silvery light of the inner cloud glittered and winked off the feathers of the steel birds as the watching crowds cheered. Odin and Bane were looking upwards, along with everyone else, and Arabella imagined them beaming triumphantly.

Overwhelmed by a sense of helplessness, she turned to Ben. 'We have to do something!' she said.

Ben was gazing up at the display like a spectator at a ballooning contest, a mysterious smile at play on his face. 'Let's just see what happens,' he said.

She turned back in time to see the Dread Eagles begin their descent.

And then – quite suddenly – *Horus* exploded.

CHAPTER THIRTY-TWO

THE
BATTLE

It was all over so quickly, it took Arabella a few seconds to realise what had happened. One moment the bird, in all its evil majesty, was floating down towards its eyrie, its prey clutched tightly in its talons – the next moment, there was a flash and a boom and a giant ball of black and orange flame billowing outwards. When the smoke cleared, *Horus* was no more.

There were gasps and screams from the watching crowd beneath as the *Nelson*, no longer supported, and with its ballonets filled with air by the pirates, lurched abruptly downwards. The crowd scattered, and Odin and Bane were forced to scramble, along with the rest, towards the perimeter, as the enormous copper hull of the battlecruiser crashed into the square.

The British crew aboard the *Nelson* seemed to respond more quickly to the new circumstances than their captors. They took advantage of the Taranites' shock by running at them en masse and pushing them off the gondola deck into the square below. Arabella stared, shivering with incredulous excitement and delight, as the British soldiers then poured overboard and began engaging the pirates in hand-to-hand combat right in front of Odin's palace. As the other twenty eagles brought their captives in to land, she saw similar fights breaking out on the deck of each airship.

'This is amazing! Fantastic!' she cried, hugging and kissing Miles, whose little chimney was puffing faster than a model steam train as his brain tried to process all this new information.

'Indeed, my lady, it appears to be a most encouraging development. But I wonder how…'

They both turned to look at Ben, who was still wearing that enigmatic smile.

'You knew this was going to happen!' Arabella accused him. Her brow furrowed as she tried to piece everything together. 'You must have planted a bomb inside *Horus* while you were building that shield.'

'Guilty as charged,' said Ben. 'The Aetheric Shield is designed to deflect external fire. It can't do anything about a bomb going off inside.'

'But why?' demanded Arabella. 'I thought these pirates were your valued customers.'

Ben shook his head. 'I'm no more a salesman than you are a flying-circus performer,' he said, before adding forcefully: 'And I'm not doing any of this for money!'

'That's not what you told me when we first met,' said Arabella.

'I had to tell you something that made sense,' he said. 'The salesman story works because everyone understands it. My real reasons for stealing the formula are – well, harder to explain.'

'Try me!' challenged Arabella.

Above them, the battle was in full swing, with booming exchanges of pistol and cannon fire, but Arabella was suddenly much more intrigued by the young man standing right in front of her.

'You may have heard of me on the spy circuit,' said Ben. 'I go by the code name Agent Z.'

'Y– you!' gasped Arabella. '*You're* Agent Z!'

'You expected someone older, huh?' said Ben, rolling his eyes. 'Tsk, I know, everyone expects that. They forget that Agent Z's only been on the scene for a couple of years. I started when I was sixteen – I was a little raw back then, of course...'

'I just can't believe it!' said Arabella, wishing she didn't sound so much like a gushing schoolgirl. But then Agent Z was a legend in her world, and when meeting a legend in the flesh it was hard to know how to behave. 'The quality of your intelligence...' she stammered. 'We all assumed Agent Z was a top French politician or general who had turned against Napoleon.'

'Yeah, well I've always had this... knack of being in the right place, you know?' said Ben. 'And I get on with people. They tend to trust me – with the notable exception of yourself, ma'am! Anyhow, over the past two years, I've found my way into the homes and offices of some of those top politicians and generals you mention. They like talking to me, some of them, and I've become privy to a few consequential secrets, which I passed on to a contact in your government.'

To Arabella's shame, her first response to this revelation was delight at the thought of how jealous Diana would be when she told her about it. Her second was embarrassment at all the rude things she'd said to him earlier. Her third was confusion.

'But if you're Agent Z,' she asked, 'why did you steal the formula for the Aetheric Shield from me?'

The smile vanished from his face, and Arabella got the sense that, for the first time, she was looking at the real Ben Forrester.

'Because I couldn't allow a weapon of that potency to fall into the hands of the British,' he told her. 'Armed with a thing like that, you guys would be unstoppable. It wouldn't be long before you'd be wanting your old American colonies back.'

'But you didn't seem to mind the French having it!' said Arabella, bristling a little at this perceived slight on her nation.

'I could hardly prevent that, since they invented it,' said Ben. 'Anyway, the French Empire is dying. The nationalists are in open revolt. This is their last, desperate throw of the dice. By the time Paris falls to the Anti-Bonapartists, I'm hoping this technology will disappear with it. Forever.'

'So then why did you sell it to Odin?'

'I used it as a lure to get Odin to trust me, so that I could destroy him. Things are playing out pretty much as I hoped.'

Arabella found herself nodding dumbly as she struggled to absorb all that Ben was telling her. How badly she'd misjudged him! From the moment he'd arrived here, he'd been quietly putting in place his plan for Odin's destruction. He was a hero as brave as any she'd come across in the adventure stories she'd read as a child – and yet he'd pretended all the while to be the exact opposite. Could he ever forgive her for the things she'd said to him?

There was no time to ask him about that, though she longed to secure his forgiveness, and hopefully, one day, his friendship. Looking back towards the battle, she saw that the British lines had failed to advance beyond the palace square, and some had been forced back towards their vessels.

'I don't think they're going to be able to take Taranis on their own,' said Arabella. 'There aren't nearly enough troops or artillery. We'll have to give them some help.'

'What can the three of *us* do?' asked Ben.

'We can destroy the cloud,' replied Arabella. 'I know where the Cloud Factory is.'

'Good thinking!' said Ben – or Agent Z, as she would now have to think of him (and it gave her a quiet thrill that she'd come up with a plan that met with his approval). 'We can rip away the cloak and turn Taranis into a sitting duck for your Royal Air Fleet!'

They headed for the exit on the far side of the terrace.

A few minutes later, they were walking along one of the many indistinguishable corridors that made up the interior of the city.

'I wonder where we are,' said Arabella

'We are on Level 34, my lady,' stated Miles.

'How does he know things like that?' said Ben, impressed.

'I have no idea,' said Arabella. 'Amazing, though, isn't he?'

Miles said nothing, but simply pointed at a sign on the wall they had just passed. It read: 'Level 34'.

CHAPTER THIRTY-THREE

THE GIRL WHO HATED

he Cloud Factory, on Level 2, had been left unguarded. Astonishingly, the factory floor was deserted – the giant copper vats puffed and hissed at each other, producing their cloud vapour, without human oversight.

'They must have roped in every available man to do battle at the top of the city,' said Ben, still breathless after their thirty-two storey descent with Miles on his back.

Once Miles had unlocked the door, Arabella cautiously entered the factory, half-expecting an ambush. When none came, she led the others over to the first of the vats. Walking around it, she spotted a small, four-spoked metal wheel near the bottom of the cylinder's enormous convex back.

'What do you suppose that is?' she wondered.

Ben looked at it. 'A valve, I guess, controlling the amount of chemical coming out of this tank.'

'If we turn the wheels on all the vats, we can stop the chemicals reaching that big cloud pump,' suggested Arabella. She pointed at the giant pillar, topped by an inverted cone, that stood at the far end of the room, the ultimate destination of the feeder pipes attached to the front ends of the vats. 'That should make the cloud disappear.'

'Your plan may work, my lady,' said Miles. 'But we don't know how long it will take for the cloud to clear, and in the meantime the Taranites might very well return and...'

'...and turn those valves right back on again,' finished Ben. 'You're right, little fella. We're going to have to think a lot more... destructively!'

He looked around and his eye immediately fell on a fire axe hanging on a wall. He strode over to it, lifted it off its mounting and hefted it in his hands. 'Perfect,' he purred. Then he went and positioned himself by one of the thick rubber pipes carrying chemicals from the vats to the pump. Holding the axe handle securely in both hands, he laid the blade on the surface of the pipe before hoisting it high above his head.

He was about to bring it down hard on the pipe, when a female voice behind them shrieked: 'Stop!'

They all whirled around, expecting to see a guard. Instead, Arabella was astonished to see Marie

Daguerre standing alone by the factory entrance. She had a gun in her hands and was pointing it directly at Ben.

'Marie?' cried Arabella, frowning.

'Drop the axe!' Marie shouted at Ben.

He placed it on the floor.

'Now step away from that pipe.'

Ben did so.

Marie swivelled her shoulders so that the gun was now aiming at Arabella and Miles. 'You two, step away from the vat. Come closer to me.'

They did so.

'That's enough,' snapped Marie. 'No closer.'

'What's going on, Marie?' asked Arabella. 'I thought we were friends.'

Marie stared at her, and Arabella noticed the girl had tears in her eyes. 'Yes, *ma chérie*, I would like to be your friend. But I cannot let you destroy these machines.'

'I don't understand,' said Arabella. 'I thought you hated the Taranites as much as I did.'

'I do,' sniffed Marie, briefly removing one hand from the gun in order to wipe her eye. 'But I hate the British even more. They killed... they killed my parents. A brutal man, a captain in your Royal Air Fleet – his name is Allenson – he tortured and killed my mother and father in front of me when I was just six. Ever since then, I have hated the British.' She glared at Arabella, her face now a mask of hate. 'I want the invasion to succeed, and for the British to feel the wrath of Napoléon. I want your nation to suffer, as I have suffered.'

She swallowed, and appeared to calm down. 'When you told me that the flagship of the Royal Air Fleet was on its way across the Channel, I knew it could only be for one purpose: to destroy our invasion fleet! I was so happy that the Sky Magister planned to capture the flagship. Even the devil can sometimes be capable of good works! But then you told me you wanted to stop him. I couldn't let you do that! I had to devise a trap. So I told you about the Cloud Factory, and then I told Commodus Bane that you were planning to break in.'

Marie's face twisted into a scowl, as she continued in a spiteful tone: 'He said to me that he would *like* to imprison you but his hands were tied by the Sky Magister, because Monsieur Forrester needed your help in making the Aetheric Shield. But I told him that was a lie. I knew it was a lie because I had overheard Monsieur Forrester telling your little automaton how much he admired his Lady Arabella, and would do *anything* to save her, even to pretend that you were a great scientist of the Aetheric Shield! I told Bane this because I had to stop you!'

When she heard this, Arabella coloured. Ben Forrester had said he *admired* her! And she'd blamed him for betraying her to Bane, but it had been Marie all along! She caught his eye and silently mouthed the word *Sorry*. Ben nodded and looked down.

'So why did you bring me water?' Arabella asked her. 'Why did you rebuild Miles for me?'

Marie sighed. The scowl faded, though her eyes still sparkled with moisture. 'I hate your country. But I find I cannot hate you, Arabella. The first time I saw you, I could see how hungry you were, and yet you offered me your food. I remembered this after Bane arrested you, and I felt... guilty. And then, when I saw what he did to you, and realised how brave you must have been under torture, I felt even worse. You are a good person. But you are *one* person. I cannot let my... feelings for you affect my sense of right and wrong. Your kindness cannot atone for all the sins of your country, not just against me but against so many of my compatriots. I am happy that Odin has captured the British strike force and that the French invasion fleet is now safe. I feel I have done my duty. But if you destroy this cloud, the strike force will be rescued by the Royal Air Fleet and continue with its mission. And then all my good work will have been for nothing.'

Marie's finger tightened on the trigger.

'Now you must be brave, *ma chérie*.'

'What are you doing?' gasped Arabella.

'I won't send you back to Bane,' said Marie, who had begun to sob. 'But I can't leave you here, or you will ruin everything... I–I will make this quick – for all three of you.'

'Listen, Marie,' said Arabella, trying to remain calm. 'Why don't we talk about this?'

'There is nothing to talk about. We could have been friends, but we find ourselves enemies. I am s—sorry for that.'

While she was saying this, her eyes were fixed on Arabella, and Ben began to sneak closer to her.

'Stop!' she screamed, and she pulled the trigger. There was a loud bang. Blood spurted from Ben's arm. He staggered and cried out, clutching his sleeve just above the elbow.

Marie's eyes were dry now, and small – like beady little pinpricks of hate. 'I will make this quick,' she snarled. 'A bullet to each of your heads, and one in the logic circuits of the automaton. But if you try any more tricks, I will aim for your lungs or stomachs, and your deaths will be slow and painful... You first, monsieur.' She raised her gun so that it pointed at Ben's forehead. He was sweating, breathing hard through his nose, lips pressed tightly together, hand clamped to his arm.

Arabella watched in horror as the knuckle on Marie's trigger finger whitened.

And then everything went wild.

CHAPTER THIRTY-FOUR

THE
UPRISING

In that second, the room rocked to the sound of a huge explosion. Plaster dust fell like fine snow from the ceiling. Marie was thrown to the floor. Arabella ran and leaped on her, wrestling the gun from her hands. At the same time, about a dozen thin figures, dressed in prisoner blue, came charging into the Cloud Factory. 'Down with the Taranite tyrants!' cried one of them. 'Up with the revolution!' cried another, and they all began whooping with excitement. Several carried guns, which they proceeded to discharge above their heads, filling the air with the crackle of gunfire and bringing down yet more plaster and chips of wood.

Arabella finally managed to prise the gun from Marie's fingers. She shouted to the nearest rebel slaves:

'Destroy the machines!' Then she aimed Marie's gun at one of the copper vats and fired. A narrow spurt of dense yellow gas erupted from the bullet hole. This was exactly the kind of simple, direct and violent call to action that the revolutionaries had been waiting for, and with a volley of jubilant war cries they turned on the cloud-making plant. Driven by bitterness against their former masters, the rebels fired their guns and swung their axes and iron bars with savage ferocity. Very soon the room was filled with high-pressure jets of purple, green, blue, red, yellow and creamy-white gas, crisscrossing and coalescing in the air as they spouted from the ruptured pipes and vessels.

In all the noise and mayhem, Arabella didn't hear the shot that killed Marie. She found her small, thin body seconds later, lying in a pool of her own blood, her eyes staring sightlessly at the ceiling. The girl had had a second gun – a small pistol, still cradled in her hand – which she had fired into her own head. Arabella recalled the moment the previous evening when Marie had appeared like an angel in her cell. The girl had saved her life, and had given her new hope in her darkest hour. With a little more time, she might have found a way of appealing to that good side of Marie Daguerre. She knelt down and closed the girl's eyes.

'Could you give me a hand?' called Ben.

Arabella looked up. He was leaning against a wrecked machine, dripping with sweat and clearly in pain. He'd ripped a strip of material from the bottom of his blue shirt and was trying, one-handedly and without much success, to bind the blood-soaked wound in his arm.

She went over and helped him with it. 'Is it very painful?' she asked.

'It's nothing,' he lied through gritted teeth. 'The bullet grazed the flesh, that's all.' He nodded towards the blue-clad rebels, still whooping and shooting up the machines. 'With luck, this little revolt, if it spreads, could tip the balance in the battle upstairs – and once the cloud's gone, the game will truly be over for Odin and co.'

'I hope you're right,' said Arabella, pulling the knot tight on the makeshift bandage. 'We should go up to the palace square and see if we can lend a hand.'

'Agreed,' said Ben. 'Come along, Miles, old buddy.'

In the corridor outside they heard echoes of screaming and gunfire coming from elsewhere in the city – sure signs that the slave uprising had spread. They made the long ascent to the top of Taranis in stages – climbing staircases up to terraces, then running along more corridors that led to more staircases and more terraces, and so on. All the while they were moving closer to the central summit where Odin's palace was situated. Each time they reached a terrace, they looked hopefully towards the cloud wall, and each time they were disappointed to see no change in it. The corridors were the most dangerous places – several times they were forced to duck into rooms and recesses, as teams of grey-uniformed armed guards came running by, en route to the battle, or to a new slave insurrection somewhere in the city.

Ben was in too much pain to carry Miles up the staircases, so the automaton was obliged to climb them himself, or at times Arabella would carry him. Either way, this made the ascent very slow, and by the time they reached the top of the final stairway and surfaced at the edge of the vast palace square, they encountered a very different scene.

Arabella, Miles and Ben found cover behind the wreckage of an armoured steam carriage and took stock of the situation. The Taranites had driven the soldiers of the Royal Air Fleet right back to their vessels and surrounded them there. The British soldiers were visible as a thin band of black hats and red tunics encircling each of the downed warcraft, hemmed in on all sides by a sea of Taranites – both grey-uniformed soldiers armed with guns and ordinary citizens wielding homemade weapons. Swooping in from above, through the haze of blue gunsmoke, came Taranite Dread Eagles, spitting fire through their open beaks at the beleaguered British troops. Arabella saw one of these birds destroyed by soldiers manning a cannon on a gondola deck – but this was a rare triumph. The British were outnumbered and outgunned by the Taranites and their defeat seemed to be only a matter of time. Yet not one of the vessel crews looked willing to surrender – it was turning into a prolonged and very bloody fight to the death.

'Stay strong, boys,' murmured Arabella.

Her ears were under constant assault by the boom of cannon, the sputtering cracks of volley guns and the moans of the injured and dying, and she felt nauseous from the acrid stench of cordite and blood – but for all the world, she would not want to be anywhere else.

'You lot! Get out from there!' barked a boot-faced Taranite sergeant, staring down at them from the top of the burned-out steam carriage behind which they had taken shelter. He was pointing a huge multi-barrelled mitrailleuse at them, so they had little choice but to obey. They emerged into the open to find themselves surrounded by a fifteen-strong unit of grey-uniformed guards.

'It's the American salesman,' grinned one of them suddenly. 'The one who blew up *Horus*.'

'And the English spy and her tin man.'

'You guys are in bi–ig trouble!' smirked another guard, drawing a forefinger across his scrawny neck.

'We could be looking at medals and promotions all round for nabbing this little lot,' the sergeant said cheerfully to his unit. 'All we need do is deliver them safely to the palace.'

Arabella, Miles and Ben soon found themselves being force-marched at the point of fifteen rifles towards the palace on the far side of the square.

'Come on, tin man! Keep up!' yelled a pimply faced young soldier, kicking Miles in the back of his legs.

'As it happens, my main component is brass,' pointed out Miles, after recovering from his stumble. 'Brass is an alloy of copper and zinc. There is no tin in me.'

'Shut up!' roared the soldier, clouting Miles over the head with his rifle butt.

Arabella looked back in alarm as her logical friend tottered for a moment as if about to keel over, before managing to right himself.

As they neared their destination, she couldn't avoid taking a closer look at Odin's palace, and concluded that it was one of the ugliest buildings she'd ever laid eyes on. The Sky Magister had obviously aimed for grandeur, but there were far too many tall turrets with steep little roofs topped with spindly spikes, and far too many tall, narrow windows with absurdly ornate architraves. It was pretentious and vulgar, in her view, and made even more ridiculous by the fact that it appeared to be sinking. The huge edifice of brick and stone had been built on top of earlier, mostly wooden structures that simply couldn't support its weight. As a result, the palace had a distinctly lopsided look, with its western side a good few yards lower than the rest of it.

Ben must have noticed her expression of distaste. 'You wait till you see the inside,' he murmured to her.

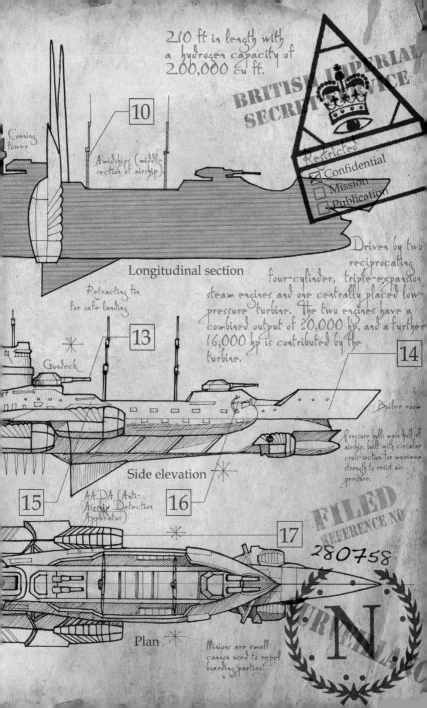

210 ft in length with a hydrogen capacity of 200,000 cu ft.

BRITISH IMPERIAL SECRET SERVICE

Restricted
☑ Confidential
☐ Mission
☐ Publication

Conning tower

10

Amidships (middle section of airship)

Longitudinal section

Driven by two reciprocating four-cylinder, triple-expansion steam engines and one centrally placed low-pressure turbine. The two engines have a combined output of 30,000 hp, and a further 16,000 hp is contributed by the turbine.

Retracting fin for safe landing

13

14

Gundeck

Boiler room

Side elevation

Pressure hulls main hull of airship, built with circular cross-section for maximum strength to resist air pressure.

15

16

AADA (Anti-Airship Detection Apparatus)

FILED
REFERENCE Nº
280758

17

Plan

Missions are small cannon used to repel boarding parties.

Tirailleur-Class Airship

Square-rigged masts

Auxiliary sails

Michaux cannon

Minions are small charges used to repel boarding parties

Gun deck

Minions

Key

1   Square-rigged masts allow the hoisting of numerous small sails that are more efficient than a single large sail. Fore-and-aft sails can be flown with a reduced crew and are efficient when working to windward.

2   A cannonball hole in a small sail affects only one sail. A hole in a large sail would eventually tear a larger area and reduce further the vessel's flying power.

3   Four rotating Michaux cannon based on the Gribeauval system.

4   Arquebus tube.

5   The Operations Room or AIC (Action Information Centre) is the tactical centre of an airship. It processes information for command and control of the near airspace or area of operations.

6   Wrought-iron hull cladding.

7   Bow armour is proof against hollow incendiary shot filled with molten metal.

8   Hold carries supplies and landing craft.

AA DA (Anti-Airship Detection Apparatus)

Concealed ironclad propellor

Tirailleur-Class Airship

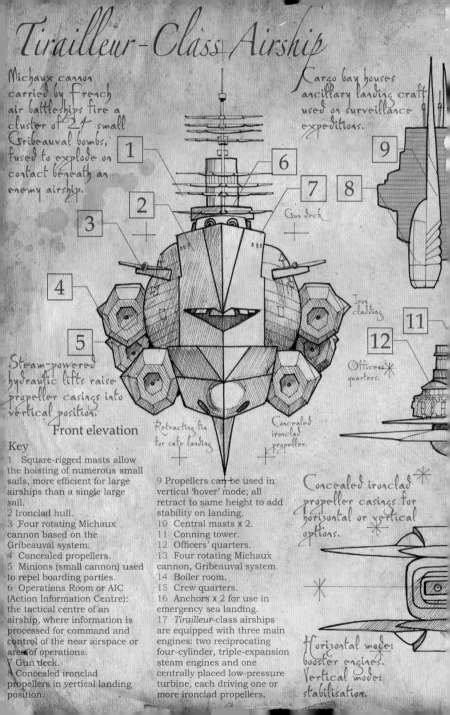

Michaux cannon carried by French air battleships fire a cluster of 24 small Gribeauval bombs, fused to explode on contact beneath an enemy airship.

Cargo bay houses ancillary landing craft used on surveillance expeditions.

1

6

2

7 8

3

Gun deck

4

9

5

Iron cladding

Officers quarters.

12

11

Steam-powered hydraulic lifts raise propeller casings into vertical position.

Front elevation

Retracting fin for safe landing

Concealed ironclad propeller.

Concealed ironclad propeller casings for horizontal or vertical options.

Key

1 Square-rigged masts allow the hoisting of numerous small sails, more efficient for large airships than a single large sail.
2 Ironclad hull.
3 Four rotating Michaux cannon based on the Gribeauval system.
4 Concealed propellers.
5 Minions (small cannon) used to repel boarding parties.
6 Operations Room or AIC (Action Information Centre): the tactical centre of an airship, where information is processed for command and control of the near airspace or area of operations.
7 Gun deck.
8 Concealed ironclad propellers in vertical landing position.

9 Propellers can be used in vertical 'hover' mode; all retract to same height to add stability on landing.
10 Central masts x 2.
11 Conning tower.
12 Officers' quarters.
13 Four rotating Michaux cannon, Gribeauval system.
14 Boiler room.
15 Crew quarters.
16 Anchors x 2 for use in emergency sea landing.
17 *Tirailleur*-class airships are equipped with three main engines: two reciprocating four-cylinder, triple-expansion steam engines and one centrally placed low-pressure turbine, each driving one or more ironclad propellers.

Horizontal mode: booster engines. Vertical mode: stabilisation.

Tirailleur-Class Airship

Class & type	9.C.A.	Power	Wind power + propellers; top speed unknown.
Length overall	210 ft	Engines	Total combined horsepower: 46,000.
Decks	10		2 reciprocating 4-cylinder, triple-expansion steam engines and a centrally placed low-pressure turbine.
Orlop deck	180 ft	Armment	4 × Michaux cannon, 18 minions
Performance		Sail plan	Light, variable, storm.

Early experiments found wrought iron superior to cast iron; wrought iron was subsequently adopted for Imperial French ironclad airships.

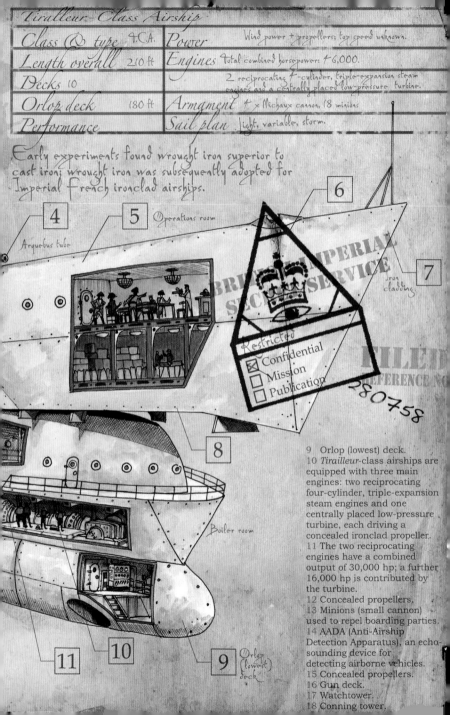

Operations room

Arquebus tube

Iron cladding

Boiler room

Orlop (lowest) deck

9 Orlop (lowest) deck.
10 *Tirailleur*-class airships are equipped with three main engines: two reciprocating four-cylinder, triple-expansion steam engines and one centrally placed low-pressure turbine, each driving a concealed ironclad propeller.
11 The two reciprocating engines have a combined output of 30,000 hp; a further 16,000 hp is contributed by the turbine.
12 Concealed propellers.
13 Minions (small cannon) used to repel boarding parties.
14 AADA (Anti-Airship Detection Apparatus), an echo-sounding device for detecting airborne vehicles.
15 Concealed propellers.
16 Gun deck.
17 Watchtower.
18 Conning tower.

CHAPTER THIRTY-FIVE

THE THRONE ROOM

The Sky Magister's throne room was situated on the highest floor of the palace, as if, having acknowledged the fact that his residence was sinking, he'd placed the most important room at the top.

When she entered, Arabella recognised the room from the magic zoetrope show. But the flickering images Miles had projected on her cell wall could not do justice to its scale, which was breathtaking. It occupied the entire floor, and was more than twice the height of any other room she'd encountered on Taranis, including the Cloud Factory. The distant hammerbeam roof was supported at regular intervals by columns the height of airship mooring towers, and on one wall was a fireplace so vast it could have comfortably accommodated the cell Arabella had spent the previous night in.

But the throne room was not just ludicrously, pointlessly and dizzyingly big, it was also a gaudy shrine to one man: every available surface of wall, ceiling or column was covered in paintings or relief carvings of Odin's face, while every recess carried a bust or life-size statue of the man. The entire end wall, behind the throne on its dais, was filled with an enormous fresco of the Sky Magister posing heroically on the prow of an armoured airboat as it delivered a massive broadside to a French *Tirailleur*. Never had Arabella seen such an obscene example of self-worship. It amused and also alarmed her that many of the walls, columns and artworks were showing deep cracks, and that the whole room was on a noticeable tilt. The palace was, like Nero's Golden House, both horribly narcissistic – and doomed!

The man himself – all six feet six inches of him – was standing by one of the windows, surveying the battle being fought in the square below. He was so still that at first she took him for another statue. But then he turned to face them and, once again, Arabella couldn't fail to be impressed by the pirate king's size and muscularity, his long coils of hair and rather beautiful, if filthy, warrior's attire. But, as before, one glance at his ice-cold eyes and cruel sneer of a mouth was enough to remind her that this man was no romantic hero.

As he stood there looking at them, it occurred to Arabella that she still had Marie's gun hidden in one of the deep pockets of her overalls. There were at least twenty armed guards dotted around the room, in addition to the fifteen who had escorted them here. She would only get one chance to shoot the man before being shot down herself – yet, if she did manage to kill him with that single shot, it might hopefully break the will of the Taranites, end the bloodshed in the square and save Operation Zeus – all with one bullet! Did she dare? She had never killed anyone before, and the thought of doing so in cold blood scared and revolted her. But the stakes, in this case, seemed to justify it. Odin's body was covered in thick leather armour, so it would have to be a shot to the head, which meant that she'd have to get closer to be sure of hitting him.

Odin smiled at Arabella and made a deep, mocking bow. 'My lady – what a pleasant surprise. The great scientist and circus aerobat, who turned out to be neither. Just a common spy. I'm almost disappointed!' He curled his lip disdainfully.

'And you!' He shook his head at Ben. 'That was quite a stunt you pulled earlier, American. For an hour or so this morning, I don't mind admitting I was scared.' He gestured at the scene below the window. 'But, as you can see, our superior numbers and firepower have started to tell. We shall win the day in spite of your efforts.

'You've made your mischief, the pair of you, trying to save the *Nelson*. But you never thought to ask yourselves why I might want to capture it in the first place. For years I've made a decent living, made my people rich and fat, on lightly defended cargo ships, filled to the gunnels with every kind of food or bauble an honest pirate can desire. Why go after a heavily armed warcraft, filled with nothing one can eat or spend, and incur the wrath of a nation into the bargain? Why? Did you ever wonder about that? Did it ever occur to you that it might not be the ship itself, or its cargo, that I had my eye on – but a certain member of its crew?'

Odin resumed his vigil at the window. 'The captain of the *Nelson* happens to be the very man who drove me up here in the first place,' he said quietly. 'Captain Allenson, whose savagery, whose devotion to the art of inflicting torment on his enemies, makes our beloved Dr Bane seem like a village priest by comparison. *That* is the man I want to capture, so that I can do to him what he did to me, only more slowly and more patiently.'

He chuckled. 'But thanks to your efforts, my young friends, he's still out there, most probably cowering inside that copper gondola, while his men fight and die to protect him. Never were so many lives expended for something so worthless.'

Odin turned to face Ben, and all traces of his smile vanished. 'You had me taken in by that salesman act, Mr Forrester. You took me for a fool... And no one does that and lives.' He turned to a guard standing next to him and murmured something to him. The guard marched away.

A moment later, a chill seemed to descend upon the hall. Before she even turned, Arabella knew, with a prickling of the hairs on her scalp, who had arrived. He stood there, framed in the entrance, the thin figure with the cloak and stovepipe hat, the one who was destined to haunt her nightmares for the rest of her life.

Commodus Bane strode into the room, accompanied by his own retinue of guards, including the bald man-mountain Arabella remembered from her two previous ordeals with the torturer. The guards were carrying a hideous-looking iron table, fitted out with hand and leg restraints. They set it down in the middle of the throne room's expansive floor.

'The American destroyed my beautiful *Horus*,' said Odin, his quivering cheeks belying the calmness of his voice. 'I trusted him, and he betrayed that trust. You know what to do, Dr Bane.'

Commodus Bane remained motionless, hands behind his back, head tilted slightly forward. His dark-lensed goggles, targeted on Ben, had the cold, calculating quality of a tarantula sizing up its prey.

'Bring him to me, please,' said Bane in his polite, educated voice.

A couple of guards manhandled Ben onto the table and closed the wrought-iron restraints around his wrists and ankles. Arabella feared desperately for him, but Ben was putting up a brave front.

Beneath the rattle and crack of gunfire from the square below, she could hear the quiet hiss of the torturer's steam-driven arm. As she knew from experience, it was when the hissing stopped that you had to start worrying.

It stopped…

The metal arm appeared from beneath the folds of his cloak, its forefinger outstretched. As if by prearranged signal, one of his guards ignited a gas torch and held it up to Bane's hand, bathing the forefinger in its blue flame.

Arabella, and perhaps everyone else in the room apart from Bane himself, stared at the finger as it slowly turned pink, then rose, then orange.

When he was satisfied, Bane nodded at the guard. The flame disappeared, and the torturer moved over to the table. He looked at Ben and said: 'Open your mouth, please.'

Hearing this, a chill ran through Arabella's insides.

Ben gazed back at Bane. His mouth stayed closed.

'Come now, don't be shy,' coaxed Bane. 'That mouth has been the making of you, young man! It won you the trust of the Sky Magister, and that's no easy feat, I assure you! I know for a fact he still doesn't trust *me*!'

This comment elicited nervous laughter around the room.

'No one ever wants to trust me! Especially around fire, for some reason!'

There was more laughter.

Ben's mouth remained closed.

Appearing to grow impatient, Bane nodded at the bald giant, who strode over to the table and placed his enormous hands over Ben's lower face. He then pulled his hands apart, forcing Ben's jaws open.

Commodus Bane bent over and peered inside Ben's mouth in the manner of a dentist. His red, smoking finger, which he was holding up in the air, gradually descended towards his victim's face.

'So,' murmured Bane, 'let's see what we can do to that silver salesman's tongue of yours to ensure that it never spins its lies again...'

Arabella could see Ben's eyes now wide open and wet with tears as the hot metal approached his mouth. She couldn't let this happen to her friend, her hero – Agent Z! She had to do something!

She glanced at Miles, her talisman, standing by her side. He was puffing anxiously, his eyes dim from all the extra calculating power flooding to his brain. But it was clear that he was powerless to save her friend.

All eyes were on the scene playing out on the table. No one saw Arabella fumble in her pocket for the gun. She pulled it out and aimed it at the middle of Bane's back. The man's lethal finger was an inch away from Ben's lips. She could see her gun's muzzle shaking and could only pray that it would find its target.

CHAPTER THIRTY-SIX

THE FIRE BIRD

rabella fired. Bane staggered, and a thin scream rose through the air, like the sound of a kettle boiling, as purple blood bubbled from a hole in his cloak near his left shoulder. He fell to his knees, clutching the wound.

'Kill her!' she heard Odin bellow, and she was suddenly surrounded by a circle of guards, their guns all pointing at her.

Arabella closed her eyes. The image of her father, quietly smiling, came to her, as she waited for the bullets to sear her flesh.

Her head was blasted by a cacophony of cracks and bangs as the guns all went off at once. She fell to her knees, yet amazingly felt no pain. Instead, surprising sounds filled her ears: whoops and cries.

Her eyelids slowly opened on an astounding scene: the circle of guards were on the floor, either dead or wounded, and charging into the room came wild-eyed men and women in prisoner blue. A wall of grey uniforms had formed at the far end, in front of the throne on its dais. The Sky Magister could be seen cowering behind this shield of bodies, looking nothing like the heroic figure in the fresco just behind him. The guards fired at the charging prisoners, and five or six fell. But more kept coming.

In the middle of the room, dangerously close to the crossfire, lay Ben, still fastened to the iron table, tugging at his restraints. Commodus Bane was nowhere to be seen. Arabella ran over to Ben. She fired two shots at close range, breaking the chains that bound his wrists and ankles. He immediately got up and pulled her down behind the table as bullets pinged around them.

'Where's Bane?' she cried. Ben pointed to a cloaked figure retreating through a concealed doorway in a recess behind a bust of Odin. They watched him disappear up a set of spiral steps.

'He's going up to the roof,' said Arabella.

Over by the dais, the Taranite guards were mounting a stout defence of their leader but, in a reversal of the situation in the square, they appeared to be engaged in a losing battle against the ever-increasing swarm of rebels.

'Thanks for saving my tongue!' Ben grinned at Arabella.

She flashed him a quick smile. 'I couldn't abide the destruction of such a charming organ.'

'From now on I shall devote its use to singing your praises,' said Ben.

Arabella blushed at this. She glanced at him just as a beam of sunlight struck his face, brightening those intense, dark eyes.

Sunlight?

They turned simultaneously to the window, and gasped. In the distance, the dense cloud wall was fragmenting. Blue sky and sunshine were breaking through. A surge of joy coursed through her, and, surrendering to an unexpected impulse, she hugged him. She felt his arms enclose her, and for a few brief moments, the battle – in fact the whole exhausting and perplexing world around her – seemed to fade. It felt… wonderful in his arms, but also daunting – like rising above a cloud bank and discovering an entirely new landscape. She wanted to explore it, but she felt like a child, lost and uncertain. She could be brave about many things, but now she was afraid – afraid, more than anything, of her own feelings and where they might take her.

A sudden crash overhead forced her out of this strange idyll. A great hole had opened up in the roof high above them, and broken beams and rafters were tumbling to the floor. Arabella's first thought was that the palace was collapsing – but then she saw a Dread Eagle come flying through the hole in the roof. It was a lot smaller than *Horus*, with a wingspan of no more than fifteen yards, but still a fearsomely big and heavy thing to come crashing through a roof above one's head. The bird hovered momentarily like a dark shroud above the combatants on the floor, who had all been shocked into a temporary ceasefire by its dramatic entrance.

A thousand steel feathers glittered darkly in the sun that pierced the disintegrating cloud outside, as the Dread Eagle glided down to perch on the edge of the dais. The hooked beak opened, revealing its thin black tongue, alive with pink coils of fire, like a stick writhing with snakes. A thick jet of flame suddenly exploded from the beak, straight into the mass of rebels. There were screams as many were engulfed. Those nearest ripped off their shirts and tried to smother the flames burning their comrades. But even as as they did so, the bird swivelled its head to the right, then to the left, curtaining the floor with yet more of the dense, yellow fire.

The screams of agony were terrible as a dozen more men and women were set alight. As the rebels fell back in disarray, the whole upper section of the eagle's head, including the hooked upper beak, flew open on a hinge at the back of its skull. Seated there, inside the eagle's cranium, was Commodus Bane – piloting the bird and also wielding its flame-thrower tongue. He was leaning to one side, wounded and probably in pain. Guards helped Sky Magister Odin into the passenger seat behind Bane, then closed up the head.

Before anyone could react, the Dread Eagle pumped its wings and took off, soaring away through the hole in the roof.

Arabella went over to see what help she could offer the wounded. Some of them were horribly burned and begging for help. She crouched by one groaning man with a severe burn on his leg while Ben poured water from a bucket slowly over the wound. Arabella was trying to find words to comfort him when Miles came up to her.

'My lady.'

'What is it, Miles?'

'Someone wishes to speak to you – a young lady by the name of Sally.'

Arabella looked up to see the girl with the chestnut hair, whom she'd briefly impersonated the previous afternoon – it seemed like a hundred years ago!

'Ma'am, I'm sorry to bother you,' said the girl, 'but some of the rebels broke into the storerooms beneath Odin's palace just now and liberated a couple of aerial steam carriages. Thay've refuelled them and now they're down in the palace square. I believe one of them is yours. You may want to go and claim it before someone escapes in it.'

Hearing this, Arabella leapt to her feet. 'Oh, my dear *Comanche Prince*!' she cried.

Ben glanced up. 'I guess the other air carriage must be mine.'

They stared at one other, and Arabella could see from Ben's face that he, like her, was anxious not to miss this opportunity for escape, yet was unwilling to leave the poor burn victims.

'You must go and claim your air carriages, or they will be lost,' said Sally. 'I'll take over with that bucket.' She gave Ben an admiring look. 'I heard it was you who blew up *Horus*.' Turning to Arabella, she added: 'And it was you, ma'am, who led the attack on the Cloud Factory. I'd say you two have done more than your fair share this morning!'

Arabella handed her the calamine lotion Marie had given to her. 'This is good for burns,' she said.

'You speak from experience,' said Sally, eyeing the scars on her arms. She smiled sadly at her. 'Go now. And good luck!'

CHAPTER THIRTY-SEVEN

THE
FAREWELL

When Arabella, Miles and Ben reached the palace square, they found it bathed in glorious sunshine. The cloak of cloud had by now almost completely dispersed. Ironically, the sky city had never looked more charming, with sunlight glittering on the hundreds of terraces, paths and gardens that formed its long, gradual incline towards the rim.

The battle in the palace square had turned decisively against the Taranites, their grey-uniformed troops now finding themselves hemmed in between a horde of blue-clothed former slaves to the rear, and a ring of red-uniformed British troops to the front. As the newly inspired British gradually pushed outwards and the rebels pushed in, the Taranites were

269

getting severely squeezed in the middle. And there was more bad news for them on the horizon…

Reconnaissance air carriages must have already spotted the newly exposed Taranis and reported its whereabouts, for an enormous flotilla of Royal Air Fleet warcraft was now visible as a line of dark blotches in the distance.

Arabella searched for her *Prince* and eventually located him taxiing slowly across the eastern side of the square. The Taranite seated in the cockpit was searching for a clear patch of ground to serve as a runway. Fearing she was too late to catch him, she launched herself into a sprint, reaching for her gun as she ran. The pilot, she noticed, was starting to panic. His grey uniform had been spotted by some former prisoners who were now advancing on him menacingly from the western side of the square. *Prince* slowed to a halt. Arabella ran in front of her craft. She planted herself squarely before the spinning propeller blades, aiming the gun at the pilot's head, and only then did she recognise who was wedged tightly into the cockpit seat: the giant with the bald head – Commodus Bane's brutal henchman.

'Get out of my air carriage, if you value your life, sir!' she cried. She could hear the ex-prisoners closing in behind her.

Under the circumstances, the giant seemed only too happy to oblige. He squeezed himself out of the cockpit, jumped to the ground and then lumbered as fast as he could across the square, pursued by a vengeful horde of blue-clad rebels.

Arabella examined *Prince* and was overjoyed to find him unharmed, but for the dents and scratches on his wings left by the Dread Eagle's claws.

Ben and Miles arrived a few minutes later. Behind them came a friendly-looking bunch of blue-overalled rebels, who were towing Ben's home-made craft using ropes attached to each wing.

'Much obliged to you, my friends,' said Ben cheerfully. 'You can leave it right here.'

'You're most velcome!' said one in a heavy German accent. 'Now you must excuse us, Herr Forrester. Our comrades require our help in ze great Battle of Liberation!' They raised their caps to him, and ran off to join the fighting on the western side of the square.

When they'd gone, Ben turned to Arabella. 'Those fine fellows worked in the warehouse where our craft were stored. They helped me overpower the Taranite bandit who was trying to abscond with this magnificent machine.'

The 'magnificent machine' looked just as ramshackle as when Arabella had first set eyes on it.

'Are you sure that thing is safe to fly?' asked Arabella doubtfully.

'Safe to fly?' spluttered Ben. 'Are you kidding me? This is an example of first-rate home-engineering.' He patted her rusty engine cowling, causing it to rattle alarmingly. To his credit, Ben managed to maintain his easygoing smile. He spun the propeller and the engine coughed like a dying man, then fell silent. Ben shrugged nonchalantly. '*Prairie Falcon* is a wonderful machine, but she can be a little, uh… temperamental.' After a few more hearty spins, the engine shuddered reluctantly to life.

Arabella turned to Miles. 'Ah well, my logical friend,' she said. 'I think it's time to pack you away.'

'Some rest, after all this adventuring, would be most agreeable, my lady,' said Miles.

'Godspeed, little fella!' said Ben.

'I wish you well, sir.'

Arabella shut off Miles's engine and placed him in *Prince*'s cargo hold. Then she climbed into the cockpit and donned her leather helmet, gloves and goggles, still usable despite the heat damage they had sustained.

Glancing once more at Ben's clattering contraption of spruce wood and bicycle chains, she asked: 'Are you sure you'll be OK, Mr Forrester? I do have a passenger seat that you are welcome to avail yourself of.'

In truth, she was sad to be leaving him, and concerned that she might never see him again. The memory of those brief, life-changing moments spent in his arms was all she would be left with.

'I'll be fine, ma'am, now don't you fret,' said Ben, climbing into *Prairie Falcon*'s precarious little pilot seat.

'Where will you go?' asked Arabella.

'To England, I think,' said Ben, as if he'd just thought of it.

'Might I see you then?' she asked, her heart suddenly pumping faster than *Prince*'s engine.

He looked at her, the smile now gone. 'I doubt it, ma'am. In fact, I think it's probably for the best if we don't see each other again. You know that I lead a certain kind of life, different from other folk, and it's a life that can't very easily include friends.'

'I quite understand, Mr Forrester,' said Arabella. She felt a horrid sinking inside, but managed to remain composed, imagining herself made of ice or stone.

'Well, it was nice knowing you, ma'am.'

'Goodbye, Mr Forrester.'

The eastern part of the palace square was empty now, and ahead of them lay almost 300 yards of cracked paving, offering a slightly perilous but perfectly usable runway.

Prairie Falcon moved off slowly, jerkily picking up speed until its wheels left the ground. As she watched the little air carriage rise above Taranis into the blue sky, Arabella bit her lip and blinked away a tear.

Comanche Prince departed Taranis three minutes later. Apart from the few remaining blobs of dense, ice-cream-like Taranite cloud, the sky was a perfect Cambridge blue. As she ascended to cruising altitude,

Arabella checked her readings and calculated her heading. Taranis had moved west during her stay there, and was now located just twenty miles south-south-east of Weymouth. She should have enough fuel to reach the coast, where she would find a convenient field in which to put down.

For now, she could relax and enjoy being in the place where she always felt happiest. After her two days in the dark and claustrophobic confines of Taranis, it felt close to heaven being up here again, in her *Prince*, soaring through clear summer skies.

Yet, if she was honest, she did not feel quite so carefree as usual – her experience in the floating city had left its marks on her, like little hooks in her heart, to go with the burn scars on her skin. Her betrayal of national secrets under torture had shaken her confidence in herself; and Bane had also planted a seed of doubt about her father's loyalty, which she would have to investigate, and repudiate, for her own peace of mind.

And Ben Forrester had, through no fault of his own, embedded another little hook in her heart – one she would have to keep to herself. There would be no taunting Diana that she had met Agent Z, no tearful confession to Cassie. This first taste of what she presumed must be love would have to remain her sad little secret. With luck, it might fade in time. Otherwise, she would learn to live with it, like a malady, and take the secret with her to her grave.

Far below, the air resounded with a series of ferocious booms. Looking down, she saw that the battlecruisers and armoured corvettes of the Royal Air Fleet were now within range of Taranis and were engaging with the big guns in the city's metal hull. The corvettes, with their matt-black, torpedo-shaped gondolas, driven by giant propellers and suspended beneath twin iron-clad gas envelopes, were a stirring sight, and one she hoped would frighten the Taranite defenders into prompt surrender.

Though the battle also appeared to be continuing at the very top of Taranis, in the palace square, she saw white flags being flown in the lower parts of the city, which she assumed were now under rebel control. Several British transport craft had docked at the rim, where large crowds of rebels and Taranite prisoners were gathering to await evacuation.

Turning her attention to the view ahead, Arabella experienced a small flutter of excitement at the sight of *Prairie Falcon* a mile or so in front. It was puttering along in its slow, erratic way, following roughly the same heading as hers, towards the Dorset coast. She hadn't meant to catch Ben up, but if he did insist on flying such a sluggish machine, what did he expect? She decided to offer him a cool, casual wave as she passed, but before she could, a startling and very scary thing happened…

CHAPTER THIRTY-EIGHT

THE ANGEL OF DEATH

The first thing Arabella noticed was a dark shape flying out of the sun behind her and heading north at tremendous speed. It flashed overhead and, with a jolt, she recognised the metallic shimmer of its wings: it was the small Dread Eagle that Bane had used to rescue Odin – and it was heading straight for *Prairie Falcon*.

Arabella opened up her throttle, determined to reach Ben before the Dread Eagle, but she was no match for its speed. It closed in fast on his rickety machine and took up position directly behind his tail. Arabella could only watch, horror-struck, as the eagle's beak dropped open and fire roared out, enveloping *Prairie Falcon*'s tail. The air carriage tipped forward, dropping into a near-vertical spiral, as flames and thick black smoke poured from its back end.

Down, down, down fell *Prairie Falcon*. Arabella raced towards it as fast as *Prince* could take her, praying that Ben had packed a parachute and was able to bale out.

Just when all hope seemed gone, she saw a figure climbing out of the stricken machine, followed by a great billowing of white cloth. The wind inflated the parachute, carrying it upwards on warm air currents, as *Prairie Falcon* continued to nosedive towards the sea far below. And there was Ben, floating serenely beneath the white, scalloped dome of his chute. He would be OK. She'd alert the coastguard on her return, and he'd be picked up.

But Bane and Odin were still there in their Dread Eagle, hovering vulture-like in the sky above him. Now they had lost everything, all they appeared to have left was their hatred, fury and desire for revenge. The bird swooped again, unleashing fire like a bright yellow scorching flare. Ben's parachute, she now saw, was burning. He was freefalling, and still too high to survive the fall – hitting water from this altitude would be like hitting concrete.

She was very close to him now – fifty yards or less – and a desperate plan hatched in her mind. It was actually a wild idea. In the whole brief history of aviation, she was sure it had never been done – and she had just one chance to get it right! A touch too fast or slow and the consequences would be catastrophic.

Again she assessed the distance between them, before putting Prince into a fast, steep dive – the fastest and steepest she could manage without losing control or blacking out. The engine screamed. The pressure on her head was like a vice, and the world became a pale grey tunnel with smoky black edges. At the count of eight she pulled back on the control stick, blinked, and peered out of the canopy window. She was now beneath Ben, as she'd hoped, but was she too close?

There was no time to adjust. He was a dark, plummeting shape just above her as her trajectory began to flatten out. He was falling towards her propeller – seemed to be falling right into it! She'd misjudged – he was going to be torn to pieces!

At the last second he seemed to bounce on a trampoline of air – Prince's own turbulence – which pushed him up and over the canopy of her cockpit. She craned her neck and saw him sprawled, unmoving, on her fuselage, just in front of the tail. Had the fall killed him?

Sliding back her canopy, she was hit by a deafening blast of air. She yelled: 'Mr Forrester! Sir!' but her voice was like a mouse's squeak in a hurricane. She reached for the sleeve of his outstretched arm, but he was too far from her. Did she see his hand moving – or was it the wind? After reclosing the canopy, she throttled back and tried to keep *Prince* as level and even as possible. She would have to perform the slowest and smoothest landing of her life, with Ben slumped unconscious on *Prince*'s back. She prayed to the gods of wind and sky to keep him safe.

Then a shadow swooped – a flash of sunlight on steel. A beak opened, unfurling its tongue of flame – a wave of intense heat struck her, and the canopy glass darkened and bulged inwards. She banked, trying to escape the Dread Eagle, forgetting in that second that she had a passenger...

Ben!

Craning her neck, she tried to see if he was still there, and with a stab of despair she saw that he no longer was. Ben was gone! Fallen into the sea!

Blinking back tears, she accelerated into a steeply ascending, twisting curve which took her high above the Dread Eagle. She felt the heat of fury surging through her, corresponding with the rising whine of *Prince*'s engine as she began looping back towards the steel bird. Predator would soon be prey. She had become a bullet of vengeance, an angel of death, homing in on her enemy. The Dread Eagle was coming into range. She moved her thumb towards the firing button as the bird's gleaming tail feathers filled her gunsights.

Blam! Blam! Blam!

With bitter satisfaction, she watched the shells from her Jennings steam cannon find their targets, blowing chunks off the Dread Eagle's tail and starting a fire in its wing. The bird flapped frenziedly as black smoke poured from its interior. Then, like a stone, it began to drop. She wished she could see a picture, or even one of Miles's magic zoetrope shows, of the scene inside the eagle's cockpit at that moment – she wanted to see the panic-struck, petrified faces of the pilot and his royal passenger as they realised where their lives of greed, hatred and brutality had ultimately led them. But perhaps such an image was best left to the imagination, for fear of disappointment. Instead she contented herself with watching the metal bird shrink beneath her into a glinting speck of insignificance.

Arabella was watching the Dread Eagle's fall, wondering if she might see the splash as it hit the sea, when she was distracted by an urgent banging on the canopy glass. She turned her head – and nearly fainted at the sight of Ben Forrester's face in her window. He was grinning at her and waving as he clung with his other hand to her port wing.

'I believe you mentioned a passenger seat that I might avail myself of, ma'am,' shouted Ben, after Arabella had slid open the canopy.

She didn't know whether to laugh or cry, and ended up doing both. This made flying difficult, as her goggles kept steaming up.

After he was safely on board and strapped into his seat, Ben thanked her. 'That was one crazy stunt you pulled back there,' he said, 'and the best darn piece of flying I've ever seen.'

'I told you that machine of yours wasn't safe,' sobbed Arabella. 'Oh, Mr Forrester, sir...' She was too overwhelmed to continue.

He leaned forward and touched her shoulder, and she briefly relinquished the controls in order to reach up and squeeze his hand.

A few minutes later, the cliffs and beaches of Weymouth Bay came in sight, and Arabella put down in a grassy meadow not far from the village of Preston.

After they'd both climbed out, they stood facing each other for an awkward moment. Ben looked a mess. His clothing was torn and he had black smoke burns and bruises on his face to go with the bandage on his arm. He stepped forward and embraced her. She hugged him back, surprised at her own fervour. 'I thought you were dead,' she whispered.

'So did I,' he said. 'But once you'd scooped me out of the air like that, I wasn't going to let go. No, ma'am! I believe I was hanging from your undercarriage at one stage!'

She didn't want the moment to end, but when she felt him pulling away, she also stepped back and tried to compose herself.

'If you like,' she said, 'we can walk into the village together and see if we can arrange some transport to London, if that is your destination.'

Ben smiled and shook his head. 'No, ma'am. I'm going to strike out…' (he looked around, and his eyes settled on a view to the north, towards some open fields) '… that way.'

'What's there?'

'I've no idea,' he said cheerfully.

'But you've lost all your supplies and equipment,' she said.

'I like to travel light.' He held out his hand. 'Well, ma'am, thanks again for what you did back there. And, for the second time: goodbye.'

She gave his hand a formal shake.

'Goodbye, Mr Forrester.'

CHAPTER THIRTY-NINE

THE CONVERSATION

By late afternoon, Arabella was back in her flat in Pimlico. She was hungry and desperate for a bath, but before all of that, she simply had to contact Emmeline. She placed a call to her office on a secure aetherwave frequency.

'Thank the gods you're alive,' said her aunt when she heard her voice.

'And Beatrice?' was Arabella's first question.

'Beatrice is fine,' answered Emmeline. 'She baled out and was picked up by a trawler an hour or so later.'

Arabella breathed a long sigh.

'You must come to Millbank House at nine o'clock tomorrow morning for a full debriefing,' said Emmeline. 'But I'm dying to know what you've been up to these past two days. Did you, by any chance, have anything to do with the dispersal of the cloud surrounding the floating city?'

'I did.'

Emmeline was waiting for her to go on, but Arabella found she couldn't. If she started speaking, she probably wouldn't be able to stop, and might just end up crying, which would never do. Finally, she said: 'Mr Forrester was there, too.'

'Mr Forrester?' echoed Emmeline, sounding puzzled.

'Ben Forrester... Agent Z.'

'Ah!' Emmeline chuckled to herself. 'Is that what the young man's calling himself these days?'

Arabella, who had been standing, now went over to the chaise longue and sat down. 'What's his real name?' she asked quietly.

'Nobody knows,' said Emmeline. 'It may well be Ben Forrester, or Jefferson Blakewood, or any one of a dozen names he's used over the period we've been in contact with him. He's a real mystery, if you want the truth... Anyway, well done, Arabella. I can't say Diana is too pleased with you. She told me you disobeyed a direct order by flying into that cloud. But I think we can afford to overlook your little act of insubordination in the circumstances. By exposing the floating city to the full might of the Royal Air Fleet, you saved the day. Once we'd brought our big gunships to bear, the pirates quickly surrendered and the strike force could continue on its way to France. I'm still waiting to hear about Operation Zeus – I'll be able to give you a full report tomorrow when we meet. But it has every prospect of being a resounding success, thanks in large part to your efforts. I hope you're proud of yourself, Arabella. I know your father would have been! Well, I'll see you tomorrow–'

'Auntie?' said Arabella before Emmeline could end the call. The mention of her father had reminded her of something.

'Yes?'

'Was there a man by the name of Captain Allenson on board HMAS *Nelson*, by any chance?'

After a pause, Emmeline said: 'Yes, I believe he was in command.'

'Is it possible that he knew my father?'

'It's certainly possible. I mean, they moved in similar circles. Why do you ask?'

'Oh, no reason... I'll see you tomorrow.'

Arabella switched off her aethercell.

For a long moment she remained seated on the chaise longue, staring at a portrait of her father on the opposite wall. Then she got up and went to run her bath.

CHAPTER FORTY

THE FLIGHT OF THEIR LIVES

Millbank House – the headquarters of the British Imperial Secret Service – was a tall, grey building in a street full of tall, grey buildings, located near the River Thames in central London. No one passing by its doors could possibly guess at the building's significance – it was anonymous and discreet, just like the spies who worked there.

At five minutes to nine, Arabella passed through the front entrance into the lobby, where she was greeted by the security guard. Then she rode an elevator to the highest floor. Emmeline was waiting for her in the corridor as the doors opened. Alongside her were Diana, Cassie and Beatrice. Arabella was overjoyed to see her fellow Sky Sisters – especially Beatrice

– but her smile melted when she observed their grim expressions. Even Cassie could barely meet her eyes.

'What is it?' Arabella cried. 'What's happened?'

'No time to explain now,' said her aunt. 'Sir George is expecting us. Follow me.'

As they walked swiftly down the corridor towards Sir George Jarrett's office, Cassie whispered to Arabella: 'I'm afraid it was a disaster, Bella, dear. The French were expecting us…'

She had no time to say more before they entered the office. Each of them took one of the austere wooden chairs facing Sir George's desk.

Sir George was standing as they came in, his black-gloved hands gripping the edge of his desk, as he treated each of them to a chilly blue stare. He looked tense and angry – Arabella could see the muscles working in his bald head.

'Greetings, ladies,' he said curtly. 'I'm sorry to have to inform you that Operation Zeus was an unmitigated fiasco.' He pressed a button on his desk and the room's lights dimmed. A white screen slid down in front of the oak panelling behind his desk. A projector of polished teak and brass, suspended from the ceiling, whirred into action and a map of the English Channel appeared on the screen. It showed a cluster of tiny red airships heading slowly south across the sea towards the coast of northern France.

'Our task force was attacked by dread eagles here, twenty miles south of Weymouth,' he said, using a white stick to point out a small representation of the floating city. 'This nearly proved a fatal blow, but thanks to sterling work by Lady Arabella, the cloud covering the city was dispersed and we were able to locate and rescue our flagship and her accompanying warcraft.'

He offered Arabella a thin sliver of a smile and a nod of approval before turning back to the map. 'The battle with the floating city delayed us by several hours, but we were still confident of success at this stage, and the task force continued on its course towards Granville, here.' He brandished his stick at the port, where black icons representing the French invasion fleet were massed. 'Unfortunately, the French must have got wind of our operation, and we were ambushed by a force of *Tirrailleurs* and *Dessalines* here, just east of Cherbourg. It was a rout. Every one of our craft was destroyed, including our flagship, HMAS *Nelson*.'

Arabella stared, damp-eyed, at the screen as a stream of black shapes darted out from the tip of the Cherbourg peninsula and encircled the airships of the British squadron like sharks surrounding a shoal of fish. One by one the British airships blinked out of existence. It looked so clinical, here on the map, but every one of those red shapes represented hundreds of men – men she'd seen fighting so bravely in the palace square on Taranis. She imagined their screams as the flaming ships plummeted into the sea.

'Were there any survivors, sir?' asked Cassie, who

was also struggling against tears.

'A handful were picked up by some Guernsey fishermen,' said Sir George. 'They're currently in a military hospital awaiting debriefing.'

'How could this have happened?' asked Diana.

'That's a good question,' said Sir George. 'There's no way the French could have planned this counter-strike without inside information. I can only conclude that someone within our ranks is feeding them our secrets. If any of you know anything that could help us root out this mole, you must tell me immediately.'

A tense silence filled the room as he looked at each of them in turn. Arabella felt the ice-torch of his stare and wondered if he suspected her of betrayal. Should she tell him what Commodus Bane had said – about her father and Captain Allenson? She decided that she couldn't. Bane was obviously a liar, and she refused to pass on slanders about her own father. As for Allenson, it made no sense for him to tell the French about a mission that he himself was leading. The man may have been a sadist, but that didn't make him a traitor.

'And what about *Titan*?' asked Beatrice quietly.

Sir George sighed and shook his head. 'We must assume, after this, that the French will accelerate their preparations for the Aetheric Shield, and for the invasion. There is no time to launch another counterstrike and, with our security so compromised, there's no guarantee that it would succeed. Our last hope rests with you, ladies, which is why I've called you here this morning. I'll now hand you over to Emmeline.'

Sir George stood aside for the leader of the Sky Sisters.

'Thank you, sir,' said Emmeline, standing up and striding over to the screen. She pressed a control on the desk and the map homed in on Granville, showing an aerial view of the French military port. Arabella made out a complex array of wharves, jetties, airship mooring towers, gun batteries, giant hangars and storage sheds.

'Sisters,' said Emmeline. 'Our mission is to infiltrate this port and then find and destroy the Aetheric Shield Generator. We don't know where it is, but we can guess it is in one of these hangars, along with *Titan* herself. I will be joining you on this mission. If we are to succeed, it will take all of our guile and expertise – not to mention a large slice of luck. We know that the flagship and shield generator will be well defended. But even the best defence can be breached if we can find its weak point. I cannot overstate the importance of this mission. If *Titan* is allowed to sail cloaked in the Aetheric Shield, no weapon we possess in these islands will be capable of stopping her. Our towns and cities will be completely at her mercy. You have to realise that nothing you've ever done in your lives is more important than this, and never has your country needed you more than now. There is no time to lose.

We must leave tonight.'

The lights went up and the screen disappeared. Arabella was stunned, and, to judge from their expressions, so were her fellow Sisters.

'Now go out and get yourselves some fresh air,' said Emmeline. 'Think about what I've said. We meet back here in an hour for a more detailed briefing.'

Arabella walked with Cassie along the Thames embankment. Neither of them could find words for their emotions. They passed pillboxes, bomb shelters, searchlights and anti-aircraft gun batteries – evidence of the city's preparation for aerial invasion – and Arabella felt the weight of expectation press ever more heavily upon her young shoulders. It seemed unreal that the future of the city, and the entire country, could depend on her and four other women.

'This is it, Cassie!' she said at last. 'This is the mission that will define our lives.'

'I feel excited and terrified at the same time,' admitted Cassie.

'Me, too,' said Arabella. 'You realise we may not survive…'

Cassie shrugged. 'It was probably never our destiny to live long lives… though I'd have quite liked to have the chance. I think… if I'd been able to, I'd love to have studied Egyptian hieroglyphics.'

'Hieroglyphics?' remarked Arabella, surprised. 'I didn't know you were interested in that.'

'Oh yes,' said Cassie. 'I've been fascinated by it since I was little. The famous Egyptologist, Professor Octavius Pinkerton, was a friend of my father's... What about you, Bella? What would your alternative life be like?'

Arabella had to give this some thought. 'It would have to involve flying,' she said. 'I couldn't live without my *Comanche Prince*. But I'd also like to learn to speak French as well as Diana, and play chess as well as my father, and witness a solar eclipse, and ride horses, and go undersea exploring in a diving suit. There's so much I'd like to do if I had the time. But if it's a case of choosing between living long enough to do all those things and dying young on a mission to save my country, it's no choice really. Saving the country wins every time!'

'I quite agree!' laughed Cassie.

'I suppose we'd better be getting back,' said Arabella.

As they made their way towards Millbank House, she glanced at her friend and saw her blink away a tear. Arabella pretended not to notice and turned her face to the sky. The clouds were white and fluffy – the breeze steady but not too strong. It promised to be a good night for flying.

THE END

A selected list of Scribo titles

The prices shown below are correct at the time of going to press. However, The Salariya Book Company reserves the right to show new retail prices on covers, which may differ from those previously advertised.

Gladiator School by Dan Scott

1	Blood Oath	978-1-908177-48-3	£6.99
2	Blood & Fire	978-1-908973-60-3	£6.99
3	Blood & Sand	978-1-909645-16-5	£6.99
4	Blood Vengeance	978-1-909645-62-2	£6.99
5	Blood & Thunder	978-1-910184-20-2	£6.99
6	Blood Justice *(Spring 2015)*	978-1-910184-43-1	£6.99

Iron Sky by Alex Woolf

1	Dread Eagle	978-1--909645-00-4	£6.99

Aldo Moon by Alex Woolf

1 Aldo Moon and the Ghost at Gravewood Hall

		978-1-908177-84-1	£6.99

Chronosphere by Alex Woolf

1	Time out of Time	978-1-907184-55-0	£6.99
2	Malfunction	978-1-907184-56-7	£6.99
3	Ex Tempora	978-1-908177-87-2	£6.99

Visit our website at:

www.salariya.com

All Scribo and Salariya Book Company titles can be ordered from your local bookshop, or by post from:

The Salariya Book Co. Ltd,
25 Marlborough Place
Brighton BN1 1UB

Postage and packing **free** in the United Kingdom